"**To prevent any *further* interruptions, he switched his phone to *silent mode*. Then he placed his phone upside down on the table near the kitchen area of the suite.**"

The next morning, Keith went downstairs to get breakfast for Whitney and himself. While he was away, the telephone rang in their hotel room. Whitney was very hesitant to answer it but figured it was Keith on the other end. Maybe he wanted to know what kind of food to bring back to the room. Wrapped in only a white bed sheet, Whitney rose slowly from the bed to answer the phone. Still naked from the night before, she answered the phone, "Hello…".

"Is this Whitney?" a female voice asked abruptly! "Yes… why? Who is this?" replied Whitney surprisingly.

"*This is Keith's wife, just tell him that his son KJ is asking for him and wanted to know when is he coming home to us?*" yelled the female on the other end! The phone call ended abruptly in a forceful hang up leaving Whitney with the phone shaking in her hand. *It was Amanda!*

SEDUCTION

He's MARRIED & His MISTRESS is PREGNANT

Curt Thomas

SEDUCTION: He's MARRIED & His MISTRESS Is PREGNANT
Copyright © 2016 CURT THOMAS UNLIMITED, LLC

ISBN-13: 9780996197793
ISBN-10: 0996197796
Library of Congress Control Number: 2016904455
Curt Thomas Unlimited, LLC, Orangeburg, SC

All rights reserved. Except for use in any review, the reproduction or utilization of this work in whole or in part in any form by any electronic, mechanical or other means, now known or hereafter invented, including xerography, photocopying and recording, or in any information storage or retrieval system, is forbidden without the written permission of the publisher:

CURT THOMAS UNLIMITED, LLC
P.O. Box 684
Orangeburg, SC 29116

SEDUCTION: He's MARRIED & His MISTRESS Is PREGNANT is a work of fiction: All characters in this book have no existence outside the imagination of the author and have no relation whatsoever to anyone bearing the same name or names. They are not even distantly inspired by any individual known or unknown to the author, and all incidents are pure invention and coincidental.

Visit us at www.CurtThomas.com
Facebook: Curt Thomas Fan Page
Instagram: @TheCurtThomas Hashtags: #CurtThomasNovel
#SeductionBook
Twitter: @TheCurtThomas

1

STARTING OVER

I guess you can say that their love started out like your typical lovebirds. It wasn't really that special to anyone else, but the person Keith fell in love with was very special to him.

The time was late December 2004. Keith had been honorably discharged for about a year from active duty in the United States Air National Guard. As a benefit to being a new veteran, he was receiving a nice check every two weeks, for a year, that was very close to what he earned while on active duty. Not bad for a young twenty-three-year-old single male. Keith even manage to obtain a college degree while serving in the military. After about year of receiving unemployment benefits from Uncle Sam, Keith knew it was time to make a change. It was awesome getting paid to do nothing but Keith knew he needed to get out and get a real job. So after six months, he moved back home with his parents to save some cash.

One day his father, Mr. James, saw an ad in the local newspaper about a job opening for security officer positions at Wake Med North Hospital in Raleigh, NC. His dad thought it would be so cool if he and Keith applied there to work. Mr. James was your average height and build for a man. He was a pastor of a very small congregation and was well-known within the community. Mr. James was in his late forties but could easily pass as Keith's brother. He looked so young to be his age. Every now and then, he would chase Keith's mother, Grace, around the house to remind her that he still had it going on. Grace was who most people said Keith resembled most because of her charming smile. She was a very quiet type of woman as long as you didn't rub her the wrong way!

Mr. James had heard of the great medical benefits that the company had to offer at Wake Med North. So that whole day, Mr. James went on and on about how great the benefits were, hoping to persuade Keith.

At the time, Mr. James made somewhat of a full recovery from a tragic accident back in the year 2000. Now he was finally back on his feet again. He had suffered broken bones in his legs, ribs, and hip. However, if you look at him now, you would have never known. He didn't even walk with a limp!

When Mr. James first mentioned the idea of working at a hospital as a security officer, Keith secretly thought it would be kinda degrading to him. "To get out of the Air National Guard and start working as a security officer? Security?" Keith thought privately. He had worn one of the best uniforms in the nation, "why would I want to go work as a security officer?" he said to himself. However, seeing the excitement in his dad's eyes and knowing he should probably get a job because the unemployment check was ending soon, Keith said, "Okay cool... let's do it pop!"

The ad in the newspaper advised candidates to stop by the security office to apply for the job. So, the next day, Keith and Mr. James got up early and traveled to hospital to apply for the job openings. Now normally an applicant would have to apply through human resources to work at the hospital, but since this security company was contracted, it was able to hire its own employees.

It was a sunny but cold day in Raleigh, NC. They arrived at Wake Med North Hospital around 7:45 am. They were greeted by the secretary who asked to have a seat. "Mr. Hightower will be with you guys shortly," said Mrs. Vanessa the office secretary. Mrs. Vanessa was a black woman in her late forties but could easily pass for late thirties. She wore small glasses that seem to balance perfectly on the tip of her nose. She was a very pleasant person and apparently knew everything that went on at Wake Med North. While the two were waiting for Mr. Hightower, a female janitor opened the door to the office. She was a black woman about five feet six and very petite in statue. As she walked in, she yelled, "Vanessa, let me tell you what I just heard about that doctor on the second floor! Girl, they say he done slept with nurse-oh… you have company I see!" Tammy (the janitor) looked over in the direction of Keith and Mr. James and with a country dialect said, "Oooh, how y'all doing?" The two men gestured back with a head-nod trying not to look interested in her story.

"Look Vanessa, you look like you have company. I'ma call you back 'afterwhile okay?" "Yes, Tammy I do." Vanessa said while staring at her. "But um, call me back in about fifteen minutes on my cell phone, NOT the desk phone!" said Vanessa. And with a small wave of a hand and smile, Tammy left the office.

To prepare to receive the application, Keith and his dad both wore ironed collared shirts, pressed khakis, and neckties. Keith's dad was sitting erect in the chair while reading a magazine about cars while Keith sat with his cell phone in his hand. Keith was scrolling through his contacts to see which girl he could chat with later that day.

Sitting in the chair holding his cell phone, Keith could not help but observe the beautiful diverse women who were entering and exiting the hospital. Since the security office was located on the bottom floor by the exit, Keith got a sneak peak of the staff. While staring out of the office window, it only took Keith a few minutes before he felt rejuvenated about working there! As he stared at the window, trying not to miss any "potentials", a tall and somewhat heavyset white male opened the door and rushed into the office as if he was running late for a meeting. With a cup of coffee in one hand and a notepad in the other, he was greeted by Mrs. Vanessa. "Good morning Mr. Hightower, we have two applicants here to see you. We have James senior and James junior." Said Mrs. Vanessa with a smile as she introduced them. Mrs. Vanessa thought it was cute for a father and son to apply together so she said "James senior and James junior" in a joking manner.

Mr. Hightower sat his notepad down on the tall counter near Mrs. Vanessa's desk and shook their hands. He took one look at the two applicant's appearance then smiled and said, "Good morning gentlemen, I'm Mr. Hightower and I'm the director over security for Wake Med North. How about both of you come into my office. I can already tell this won't take long!" Mrs. Vanessa knew that look on Mr. Hightower's face. It meant that he really like what he saw in Keith and his dad. Once Mr. Hightower discovered that Mr. James was a pastor and Keith was a veteran, their interview was over! Mr. Hightower hired them both on the spot! Since it was Friday, he decided to give them a start date of the following Monday! Keith got assigned the graveyard shift and his dad second shift.

Working as a security officer for Wake Med North would the beginning of something special for Keith. It was the beginning of something that would change his life forever.

2

NEW FLAME

It's Monday and there he was, his first night on the job at the hospital. Wake Med North had a decent group of security officers. The officers there were mostly older in their late forties and fifties compared to Keith who was still in his mid-twenties. Keith was not only the newest officer on the block, but also the youngest. He was young and unapologetically single! Keith was naturally a flirt. He really knew how to make anyone like him with his charismatic and charming personality. Keith was a member of a college fraternity too. The men of his fraternity had a reputation of being the kind of brothers that were always clean-cut, classy, sexy, "pretty", educated, very romantic but the freaky-in-bed kind of brothers. They were known for pleasing and stimulating women in so many ways including mentally, sexually, and of course orally.

Within his first week working there, Keith overheard talks from his co-workers that he was causing the topic of many conversations among the female staff. They were asking the other security officers

"Who's the new guy?"

"He look too young to be a security officer!"

"What's the scoop on him?"

"Is he single?"

"Is he married?"

"Have any kids?"

"Does he have a car?"

As a military man and frat boy, Keith was fairly used to the attention. He didn't let their chatter go to his head. He would go around the hospital doing security checks and show his dimples just to start trouble. He would walk through the nurses' stations and hallways as if he were a *demi-god*, half 'god' and half human. Keith had a deep voice, a chiseled face with a dark mustache and beard, almond brown skin tone, low-cut waves for a hairstyle, broad shoulders, but most importantly, he was fit.

Keith's favorite part of his new job was checking on the staff: the cooks, doctors, administration, janitors and nurses. If they worked there, he checked on their well-being. Just doing the normal things that a security officer is supposed to do within his job description. Every now and again, Keith would stop and speak with the nursing staff on each floor. His dimples were not too deep but the they seemed to love them! They were kryptonite and he knew it!

As a young single man who owned a car, with no kids, he felt like he was the biggest fish in the entire hospital. Keith had so many beautiful women to choose from whom were not only beautiful but they were smart, classy, business-minded, and most of all getting PAID! He met women who were traveler nurses, who have traveled the nation just to make $10,000 every two weeks. Keith met women who worked in physical therapy, X ray, medical assistants, the lab, and human resources. Women who worked outside the hospital, in the pharmacy, the cafeteria, in medical records, in IT, the list went on and on.

About two weeks later while working graveyard shift, Keith got a phone call on his cell phone from his supervisor, Sergeant Anderson. Sgt. Anderson was a dark-skinned brother about five foot ten and weighed about two hundred and eighty pounds. He was a laid-back kinda supervisor who didn't bother anyone unless he needed to. While on the phone said, "Hey Keith, can you please go on the third floor for me? There's a nurse up there that wants to speak to you, she thinks you're so cute. I told her that I would give you the message. She's about five feet one or so, somewhat thin, caramel skin tone and she's wearing micro-braids…I think. Now Keith, just go up there and say hello! You don't have to do anything special, just make sure you tell her I sent you."

While listening to Sgt. Anderson give the description of this nurse, Keith was rubbing his chin and smiling to himself. Keith said, "Wow, that's too funny, but okay I'll go just to say *hello*..." After he ended the phone call with his supervisor, Keith thought it was kinda funny how Sgt. Anderson was so damn descriptive of this nurse. He wondered if his supervisor liked her too, but he just laughed it off while on the way to her floor.

Normally Keith would take the staff elevator just for the opportunity to talk with the employees, but this time he took the stairs. On his way up the stairs, he checked all the doors in the stairway to make sure they were secured so that he could have extra time to speak with his *crush*. He finally arrived on the fourth floor. He opened the door just as he normally would open it, but this time, he opened it with much more class. Keith made sure that his shoes were shined, his pants straight, and that his belt was aligned just right with the gig-line flushed with his shirt. His hair was brushed so his waves on *fleek*! Keith was GQ ready.

He walked onto the *fourth* floor. He spoke as he passed several nurses. He made sure he was as charming as Denzel Washington. His teeth were as white as Morris Chestnut. While looking for the nurse his supervisor spoke of, he walked down the hallway towards the nurses' station pretending he was doing his normal rounds. Keith noticed that the floor was very quiet. It must have been lunchtime for the nurses because only one nurse was sitting at the nurses' station. Then he saw a young woman down the hall who had her back turned towards him. She fit the description that his supervisor told him. She was about five foot one and maybe a hundred pounds soaking wet. Her hair was black and in micro-braids style (skinny twists). She had a very nice caramel skin complexion as described by his supervisor. Then it dawned on Keith, he had seen her before on this floor. He vaguely remembered catching eye contact with this nurse a few times when he made his rounds. He had made her smile during recent conversations not too long ago. Keith thought to himself, "shhhiit, this is going to be too easy!"

This young lady was facing the sink and washing her hands as if she had just finished giving nursing care to a patient. Since her back was turned towards him, Keith figured that he could just sneak up behind her and tap her on the shoulder to say hello. He figured that she would slowly turn around like *Cinderella*, see her *Prince Charming* standing in front of her, and instantly fall in love with him.

He built up the courage and approached her while she was still washing her hands. She was the only nurse on the hallway. No techs or patients were near her either. He walked up to this beautiful woman and gracefully tapped her on the right shoulder. To his surprise, the petite nurse quickly turned around and almost punched him in the face! This tiny little woman literally almost cold-clocked him! Keith leaned back as if he was Neo from *The Matrix!* Shit, she was NOT the same woman that he initially thought! This was obviously a totally different woman who matched the exact description. By this time, Keith was so dazed and confused at what had just happened. This lady was the exact same height, had the same hairstyle, the same skin complexion, but she was NOT the woman he was supposed to meet.

Keith had never seen this woman before, ever! Even though she almost punched him in the face, Keith immediately liked her attitude. She had a feisty attitude, she had spunk, she was obviously educated but went into straight *angry bitch* mode and he liked it!

After the near close-quarter-combat session was over, she looked at him with a face that was once full of rage but now a quiet smile. She said with a smile, "Boy, don't you ever sneak up behind me like that; I'll punch you straight in your face!" She had the attitude and beauty of a Jada Pinkett Smith. As embarrassed as Keith was, he just smiled, rubbed his chin with his right hand, and hung his head in shame. Keith tried to explain to her that it was a *huge* coincidence and that he was looking for someone else. He told her this in the deepest voice possible.

Keith apologized to her and extended an opened hand to introduce himself. "My bad, I'm Keith...Keith James." he said. She reached out her hand to shake his hand, smiled and said, "Keith is it? Nice to meet you. I'm Amanda Scott." She was gorgeous! Her complexion was radiant pecan brown. Amanda had French manicured nails, perfectly arched eyebrows, and an acne free face that lacked make up but shined from natural beauty. Once she calmed down, her voice was soft and angelic. She spoke in a very articulate and elegant manner...very elegant for a twenty-six-year-old who looked about nineteen.

Even after that explanation, Keith still felt embarrassed. He honestly thought about running off the floor as though he had an emergency call or something. Keith then looked over his shoulder at the staff that were gathering around the nurses' behind him. One of the nurses yelled, "Tiny, you okay darling?" while laughing. The nursing staff, about five in number, were smiling at each other as if they knew the two had found love. That moment was the beginning of something special for Keith and Amanda. They both smiled at each other for a few seconds (but to Keith it felt like five minutes) then they parted ways.

After leaving her, Keith entered the nearest stairwell and immediately called his supervisor! He began the conversation by fussing at him for sending him to the wrong floor!

"H-e-l-l-o, this is security…" His supervisor answered the phone sounding half asleep. "Man, you sent me to the wrong floor!" Keith said while laughing. He said, "What do you mean the wrong floor? Wait, which floor did you go to Keith?"

"I went to the fourth floor like you said!"

"Keith, I said she works on the *third* floor, not the fourth!" He said "Damn…you're right man. You did say the third floor didn't you?" Keith said laughing. Keith met up with him later that night to fill him in about what had occurred with the new mystery woman on the fourth floor and even he started laughing at Keith!

3

SOUTHERN GIRL

It seemed like time had swiftly passed by on the graveyard shift for Keith that night. Before he knew it, Keith had finished his routine checks, filled out all the reports needed for the next shift. It's morning and it was almost time to clock out. The weather was very cloudy with loud sounds of thunder and raining heavily. Keith looked at his watch; he knew that Amanda would be getting off work soon. He really enjoyed his brief conversation with her and wanted to get to know her a little more. Considering Keith was getting to know how things routinely worked at Wake Med North, he knew around this time most nurses would be leaving to go home. He knew that most times they would take the elevator down to the ground floor where his office was located.

Time was ticking; Keith hurried back to the security office to position himself to catch a glimpse of Amanda once again. He didn't want to appear *stalk-ish* or creepy, but he wanted to meet her in the hallway to chat with her again even if it was only for a second. If he timed it right, he would walk out of the door of his office right before she got near the exit of the hallway to the parking lot. Keith realized how hard it was raining outside, so he went into his locker and fetched his favorite umbrella. He wanted to be a true gentleman towards his new crush and maybe... just maybe he could win her over with his smooth charm. Keith's umbrella was decorated with his fraternity colors of red and white. As corny as it sounds, Keith wanted Amanda to see it so that she would know that he was a distinguished man who wore his letters proudly. He knew she obviously had a college degree and knew the image and reputation his fraternity.

Keith looked at it his watch, it was time. He went back into his locker and grabbed his handheld mirror and brush. He starting brushing his hair slowly yet methodically being sure not to interrupt his wave patterns. Keith placed his brush and mirror back into the locker and walked out of the security office to appear as natural as he could.

Just like clockwork, Amanda and another nurse turned the corner and made their way towards the exit door. It was one of the nurses who witnessed the first encounter of Keith and Amanda on the fourth floor. Nurse Emma was an older short white female who had been a nurse for over thirty-five years. She was a widow and always treated "Tiny" like her daughter.

Lights, camera, ACTION! There Keith was, standing by the security office door looking as studious as Taye Diggs as he leaned against the security door pretending to be busy reading a small notepad. As Emma and Amanda approached him, he greeted them.

※

"Well, hello again! Wait... don't swing!" He said while dodging and laughing! Nurse Emma started laughing and said "We don't call her "Tiny" for nothing... she's a little stick of dynamite! I was coming to help beat you up if she needed me too! Anyway, I'll see you back here again tonight Tiny! I'll leave you two love birds alone! Lord, it's raining cats and dogs outside! Bye y'all!" Amanda and Keith laughed at the humorous comment from Emma as she unfastened her umbrella then exited the door.

Keith turned and looked back at Amanda. Realizing that she was also ready to go he said. "Listen Amanda, I sincerely apologize again for last night. It probably wasn't a good idea for me to just walk up behind you like that."
She laughed and replied, "Yeah, you're right! I'm from Georgia... we don't play that!"

He laughed and said, "I tell you what, why don't I make it up to you? It's raining pretty heavy outside. I'd hate for you to get all wet. How about using my umbrella to keep yourself dry? Just keep it until I see you next time. Truthfully, I'm only letting you use my umbrella because I think you're pretty and your hair looks nice..."

Keith said this to her as sexy and as smooth as he possibly could. He made sure his voice was baritone while he gently rubbed his beard. As he was talking to Amanda, he looked down at her purse; she actually had an umbrella. It was pink and green and had the words of her sorority written all on it. She looked at Keith's umbrella and sarcastically replied,

"Boy, I don't want to use that ol' umbrella with them colors on it."

She said this with a flirtatious smile and tone of voice as if she was somewhat surprised that he was Greek affiliated too. This was not the way Keith had imagined the conversation would go but *he liked it*. She was flirting back with him and he knew it. Realizing that was showing interest in him, Keith said, "Why are you so damn feisty? Fine, you don't have to use my 'pretty' umbrella. I know you secretly want to though. Go ahead then with your little pretty self. I'm wanna to get you breakfast one morning. I really am sorry about last night. Will that be alright with you?"

Realizing that her eyelids were beginning to match her heart rate, "Whatever, but yeah, that would be fine." She replied with smile and walked towards the exit. Keith stood there as if his feet were glued to the floor. He smiled and watched her walk away. He was admiring her walk because Amanda was slightly bowlegged and her ass seemed to just move perfectly with each stride. When she was finally out of Keith's sight, he threw his keys up in the air and caught them in excitement! He was getting the feeling that she was kinda interested in him. Keith then smiled to himself and whispered, "Yep, Ima *hit* that and she don't even know it yet!" Keith had a habit of being partially conceded at times and that was one of those moments.

The crazy thing was that while talking to her on the fourth floor, Keith never looked to see if there was a ring on Amanda's finger or not. Luckily for him, there wasn't one. To Keith, she was now someone he had to have in his life. Her attitude and personality made her so irresistible to him. Keith had been "around the block" with his share of ladies for a while but for some reason Keith felt deep down inside that Amanda maybe the *one*. That was a bitter but sweet pill to swallow considering he was still somewhat a player.

From that day on, Keith became excited about going to work at the hospital. Although he was being paid to work, the only person he really came to see was Amanda. Keith had to drive twenty-eight miles to get to Wake Med

North. For the most part, the entire twenty-eight-mile drive would be thoughts of her. Every night that he had to work, he hoped that Amanda would be working too. Keith got to know the kind of car she drove to work because he patrolled the parking lot from time to time. So if he saw her car in the parking lot after a certain time, he knew she was working.

One night while patrolling the parking lot, he saw Amanda's car parked in the parking lot. Keith built up the courage to finally ask for her number. While doing his floor check on the fourth floor, he saw Amanda alone at the nurses' station. All the other nurses were either at lunch or attending to other patients. Keith started a conversation with her.

"You sitting at this desk like you're the boss or something!" said Keith to Amanda.

"Well, for your information I am the boss, I'm the charge nurse tonight. Anyway, don't you have better things to do than to just walk around like you're God's gift to women?" sarcastically replied Amanda.

The two went back and forth for a few minutes flirting with each other. Keith seeing that other nurses were coming down the hall towards the nurses' station decided to ask Amanda for her phone number. She looked at him and said, "...and what if I said no?" "You can say no if you want to but how am I going to contact you when I get that breakfast I promised you?" replied Keith with a devilish grin.

She shook her head, smiled and wrote her number down for him on a blank notepad. They exchanged phone numbers as if it were a drug deal between a drug dealer and a pot-head. The two began texting each other. He would text her while she worked just to flirt with her. Making sure not to text her at the busiest time of her shift, he would wait until 2 and 3 a.m. That time of morning was normally very slow and the time most of the patients would be asleep. It was also the time of morning when staff took their lunch break. Perfect time to exchange conversations!

During their initial early morning conversations, Keith found out Amanda and her boyfriend of five years had recently ended their relationship. She was single now and somewhat ready to mingle. Keith knew five years was a very long time for anyone to be involved with someone. Hell, five years and you're pretty much married to that person. However, Keith's thought was if she's moving on, then he was more than happy to oblige her.

Al Green said it best when he mentioned in his song that nothing good happens around three in the morning. Considering that around 2 a.m. or 3 a.m. were the times Keith made his routine walk-thru on Amanda's floor, he knew that she would probably be either eating or surfing the internet aka shopping if her workflow was slow. Then the two became very comfortable texting each other flirtatious texts. Keith would text *seductive* messages he knew would get Amanda aroused while at work. For example, Keith would text "Damn, I'm bored right now… I wish we could meet in the supply room so I could force you to turn around, pull your scrub-pants to your ankles, cover your mouth with my hand and fuck you *doggy-style* while you lean against the wall." Those were the kind of messages he would send to her that time of morning. Keith always had a way with words. Amanda didn't think Keith was all *talk* either. She saw the way he would look her up and down while simultaneously licking his lips as though he was sexually engaged with her. She knew a "talker" when she heard one but she had a feeling that Keith wasn't just a talker, he was definitely a *performer.*

Keith always arranged his words in a way that would have her so wet and horny from reading them. Keith knew this because when he would text her something sexually explicit, she tried not to catch eye contact with him. And whenever she did, she would get all flustered by dropping ink pens or papers all over the floor trying her best to ignore him. Too funny for Keith at times seeing her squirming to keep her composure whenever he was around.

Over time, the two had been flirting with each other to the point where their conversations were beginning to become even more intense. They were becoming closer than friends but not yet in a relationship. A few weeks went by and one morning, Keith decided to text Amanda to see if he could get her breakfast from a local family-owned restaurant near the hospital. It was the kind of restaurant that was located in a small building where the owner was the cook and the family members were the staff. The kinda place you could go and they will know what you want before you had a chance to give them your order. Keith and Amanda had spoken of that restaurant in a previous conversation. After all, he did promise her breakfast weeks ago. He texted her around five a.m. and asked her what she wanted to eat. He didn't know if she was a vegetarian or some serious picky eater. She was so petite and looked like she only ate lettuce and fat-free dressing 24/7. When she finally replied, she texted that she wanted grits, scrambled eggs, crispy bacon, toast (no butter) and believe it or not corn-beef hash. This Georgia girl, with all that education and nice petite body... ate grits, eggs, bacon and corn-beef hash? Keith knew he was in love now!

Keith's cell phone rang a few minutes later. It was Amanda on the caller ID. Keith was hoping she wasn't reneging on the breakfast. He knew he was a bit freakish with some of the texts he sent to her while at work that night. After a slight pause and biting his bottom lip, he answered the phone. When he answered the phone, she sounded like she was running or stumbling over something. "Why does it sound like you're running a damn marathon? What are you doing?" Keith sarcastically asked. Realizing she was a bit out of shape, Amanda calmed down by taking a deep breath by turning her head and exhaled away from the phone. Then she replied, "Oh, I was walking up the stairs in my apartment... stop being nosey!" She told Keith that she had left work early and was wondering if he could bring the breakfast over to her apartment.

"Okay, cool, well send me your address so I'll know where to go!" "Okay!" They ended the call and she text her address to him. She quickly took a short shower to freshen up from the long twelve-hour shift. Keith plugged her address into his GPS navigation system, grabbed breakfast and was now on the way to her apartment. On his way there, Keith made sure he re-brushed his hair. He was determined to look like he just stepped out of a GQ magazine. Keith sprayed a tiny amount of his favorite cologne, *Escape* from Calvin Klein while on the way. He didn't want to over-do-it with the cologne. It took him roughly ten minutes to arrive to her apartment. Keith pulled into the parking area. He looked around and thought her duplex was pretty nice. The apartment was for only three tenants, so Amanda had plenty of privacy. The colors of the apartment were acorn brown on the top half of it, which was made of vinyl and the bottom half was decorated in red brick. All three of the front doors of the tenants were white with a glass door. The grass was freshly cut. He was glad to see that Amanda lived in an area where there weren't any thugs walking or hanging out of doors. Keith was even more amazed that she found a nice place so close to Wake Med North.

After parking his car, looked into the rearview mirror and yelled, "Damn dude... you're fine as shit!" He said this as if it were his mantra or something. Reaching over into the passenger's seat, he grabbed the breakfast in one hand and his phone in the other.

"I'm here woman... open the door!" Keith texted to Amanda.

"I know... I smell you! " replied Amanda jokingly. For some reason, in their talk, she always told Keith that he was stank. Not as in a funky smell, because she loved the smell of his cologne. When at work, Amanda always knew when Keith was either on her hallway or had been on the floor because of the distinct smell of his fragrance.

Moments later, Keith strolled toward her apartment door with food in one hand and drinks balanced in the other. As he approached her apartment, the door opened and Amanda peeked her head out. She watched this nice looking brother walking up to her door still in his security uniform. His shoes were still shiny and his uniform still looked pressed. She always thought it was funny how his uniform shirt stayed crisp and his black pants always had a crease even after a long night of working.

She opened the door and invited Keith inside. Amanda was wearing grey sweats, a grey tank top, and white Hello Kitty fuzzy slippers. Keith walked in, sat the breakfast on the black coffee table and looked around. The smell of lavender filled the atmosphere. Amanda's tanned carpet looked freshly vacuumed. She had a black leather sectional sofa and a love seat to match. The television was a nice flat screen TV resting on a glass stand. Amanda had paintings of exotic animals and some photos of family members flushed against the white walls in the living room. Not too bad for a single woman thought Keith.

They had their first unofficial date at her apartment over breakfast. The two chatted and watched the morning show together. They talked for a little while then Keith left. They both were pretty exhausted from working all night. Plus, Keith was being gentleman even though he had a hard dick as he watched Amanda walk around the apartment with only a tank top, no bra, and sweats that seemed to barely hang on to her petite, but curvaceous hips.

4

LOVERS & FRIENDS

A few weeks passed, Keith and Amanda were still flirting with each other whether in person or by texting at work. One morning, Keith called Amanda because he knew she would be getting off work soon. The phone rang and she answered.

"Hey! I'm about to give shift-report in a few minutes so I can get out of here… what's up?" answered Amanda.

"Hey, I'm getting off soon too… are you hungry?" Keith asked.

She smirked and replied, "Yeah, I'm actually starving!"

"Okay then, I'll get breakfast for you. What do you want besides my body? Nevermind, I know… what you want;

grits, scrambled eggs, bacon and corn beef hash right?" He said in his smooth voice.

She said "Yeah, that's exactly what I have a taste for… wait, don't act like you got me figured out!" She said while laughing sarcastically.

"Yeah, yeah whatever! How much time do you need before I can come over and bring it to you?" He asked.

"Just give me about an hour, then you can come on over. I have to shower to get these nasty germs off of me." Amanda replied.

※

Keith ordered *the usual* from the same restaurant then headed over to Amanda's apartment. Keith popped a mint into his mouth, brushed his hair and said his normal mantra before pulling into Amanda's driveway. Amanda could hear Keith parking because his loud SS Camaro vibrated her apartment walls. She hurried and put on the last bit of make-up, brushed her hair and headed downstairs to meet Keith at the door. Keith checked himself in the mirror one last time then stepped out of his car. He walked around to the passenger's side, grabbed the breakfast and walked slowly towards her apartment door doing his balancing act again. Keith had his hands full but managed to ring the doorbell.

Amanda peeped outside her front window trying not to laugh too loud at Keith. She was amused because he was trying to balance the food with both hands while using his chin to hold the drink cups, all while trying to look cool. Keith was literally struggling, but managed to ring the doorbell again. The door gently opened. *Damn, it took you long enough*, thought Keith to himself. He stood frozen hoping not to embarrass himself by dropping the food. He slowly raised his eyes. At first, he was only able to see her freshly manicured feet as she stood in the doorway. Then as he raised his eyes a little more, he saw her ankles, then calves, then her thighs, and finally... the bottom of what looked like a black silk robe. Amanda was dressed all in black. Not dressed in black as if she was going to a funeral either. She was dressed in an all-black see-through lingerie; a black Victoria's Secret bra, black *see-through* underwear, and a black *see-through* lingerie robe. She was so beautiful and laced with finery. Her radiant caramel skin tone accented the black tasteful lingerie that complimented her warm smile, which greeted Keith at the door. She wore a small diamond belly ring to accent her lightly carved abs. Her toenails were French manicured. And the sweet lavender fragrance of her body lotion also greeted Keith at the door.

Keith could not see her entire performance at first because his head was looking down trying to balance the food and drinks with his chin. However, when the door fully opened, and his eye raised, he saw her golden shaven legs and then the see-through panties. When he was able to see her whole statue, Keith started stuttering and said, "Ah-ah, you-you-you wanted breakfast right? Ah-ah-ah… damn!"

She looked at him, smiled, tilted her head and said, "Huh? I don't understand… what did you just say?"

Keith, still stuttering while licking his lips said, "ah-ah, I got the ah-ah breakfast."

Gently biting the tip of her right forefinger with her teeth and running her finger down her bottom lip, she smiled. Then she said, "Well, are you going to come in or what?" Keith walked inside trying not to trip over the entrance step. He sat the breakfast on the coffee table. By this time, Keith's dick was harder than a missile! Keith picked up Amanda's plate and held it towards the direction of Amanda expecting her to get it so he could leave. Keith didn't want to appear to be *thirsty*. What he didn't know was that Amanda was secretly falling for him too. They have been friends for a while now and she wanted to surprise him with some lingerie she recently got for herself a few weeks ago.

She reached out and slowly placed the breakfast back down onto the table. She gently grabbed Keith by the hand and slowly walked him up the stairs. Amanda walked up the steps as if she was a model displaying her body for Keith. Once they both reached the pinnacle of the stairs, she turned towards Keith and bit down on her bottom lip. She simultaneously removed her black robe without losing eye contact with him. Then welcomed him into her bedroom. She made sure to have the curtains shut to block out the morning sunrays. The curtains were very thick so it was extra dark in the room. While soft music played in the background, only small candles illuminated the bedroom. Amanda turned around, stood on her toes and softly kissed Keith on his lips. While they exchanged kisses, Keith gently stroked his thumb against her bottom lip then he grabbed her waist with one arm. Still kissing, he caressed her right side of her face. He whispered in her ear, "you are so damn beautiful" as he felt her heat against his cheek. It was their first kiss and it was so electrifying! They glanced at each other for a few seconds. Their eyelids matched their heart rate. They closed their eyes again and started kissing passionately again. With their eyes closed and hearts opened, they entered the beginning of ecstasy.

Keith gently laid her small, soft, petite body down on her back onto the bed while he stood next to her. He stroked his finger against her bottom lip and gazed upon her angelic body. He licked his lips as he anticipated tasting her universe. "Be gentle… it's been a while", whispered Amanda.

He looked over into her eyes and devilishly responded, "By all means babygirl but just so you know, *I aim to please….*" As his voice replied in a low growl that made Amanda both calm and aroused. Heated by his gaze, Keith leaned down towards her and started kissing her soft lips again. With every soft kiss and moan was the exchanged of passion and energy from the long anticipation of them uniting.

After the exchange of vibrant kisses, Keith slowed his rhythm of kissing to a slight pause, leaving her bottom lip moist and wanting more. Amanda wanted more, so much more. Keith could tell from her anticipation that it had been a long time since she had been kissed in that way. He could tell that maybe she was used to the *usual* and mundane kind of kissing. You know, the type of usual kissing that a woman could get use to from a man who *devalued* his woman's need for adventure and unfulfilled fantasies because he has gotten use to her. However, Keith was anything but usual. He was about to break Amanda off righteously and he *knew* it.

He kissed and licked her lips as he moved down her neck towards her collarbone. There was no stopping them now. They both wanted each other so badly. He kissed her collarbone and slid his warm wet tongue down her chest towards the middle of her black Victoria's Secret bra. Her heartbeat quickened! Like an award-winning magician, Keith reached his right hand behind Amanda's back and unsnapped her bra without missing a beat while his tongue continued to lick her mid-chest. Her bra released slightly. Without being told what to do, Amanda raised her arms above her head, allowing Keith to slide his hands up against her lavender scented skin. He ran his hands under her bra and gently removed it over her head. When his hands reached her hands to remove her bra, he joined both of her hands together and held them together with one hand. With the other hand, he slid it down her right arm, passed her elbow until his hand returned to her chest. He continued to kiss her chest while gently cupping her right breast. As he kissed her chest, he could taste the lavender fragrance of her lotion now imprinted against his tongue. He leaned over to her right breast that was cupped and gently squeezed it.

With her nipples puckered in anticipation of his warm wet tongue, he leaned towards it and began doing mini circles around them. Keith licked the tip of her raised nipple and her areole as though he was licking the tip of a cherry lollipop. Amanda seemed to be hypnotized by the long forgotten sensations than ran through her body. She arched her body and released a quiet moan while he tantalizes her body. The delicious moaning was letting Keith know that he was introducing her into ecstasy. Amanda's pulse was rapidly increasing with every touch of Keith's tongue. Each touch sends tasty shivers up her spine. Her *liquid moisture* couldn't be contained as she felt it saturating through her new panties. After kissing, licking, and gently squeezing Amanda's breasts, Keith kept performing down towards her belly button. Could she really admit her deepest longings to be echoed against her ceilings? She quietly questioned to herself. Yet she had already trusted him with far more. The way he bypassed her belly button, as he continued downwards, was as if he was saying a quick *hello* and *goodbye* to her belly button. Only teasing her with two small kisses and a gentle lick because that was not his destination. The smell of lavender body lotion filled his nose as he licked down towards her bikini line. Goose bumps rose and sensations of pleasures showered all over body. Then Keith abruptly paused... only to remove his watch and to roll up his sleeves. He reached over and placed a small bath towel between Amanda's butt and the bed sheet. He was about to *taste* all--of-her and didn't want anything to be in his way. Amanda's heart rate was beginning to go through the roof! *Is this really about to happen?* She thought to herself. As she thought this, Keith slowly and gently reached over to remove her panties. "Shiiittt, I guess so", she sarcastically answered herself while simultaneously raising her butt off the bed so that the panties could slide off effortlessly.

As she prepared herself to be pleasured, Keith began kissing from her bikini line down towards her shaved *heaven*. Amanda had gotten a Brazilian wax job the day before. *What a way to be prepared Amanda!* She silently complimented herself. There was not a single hair in sight. Keith thought to himself, damn... *her pussy is prettier than her face*, as he beheld her universe. As he kissed around the inside of her bikini line, he could literally see that her clit was swollen and throbbing from his kisses. As he got closer to it, Amanda arched her back in anticipation of his tongue resting on her clit, but instead Keith simply bypassed it. He started kissing her inner thigh and slowly licked it up and down. This was turning Amanda on so much and Keith knew it! He was in charge and wanted her to know it. Then he reached over with his right hand and used two fingers to slowly expose her clit. He licked the outer parts of his lips one last time as he beheld her universe. She smelled divine, like the perfect mixture of natural fragrance and lavender body wash, or the most seductive scent in the world.

Finally, after a long anticipation, Keith stuck his tongue out like a snake and began vertically licking her clit in a flicking motion. Keith was definitely in the driver's seat now. As Usher's song, "Can you handle it?" played in the background, Keith began stroking his tongue onto her clit to the beat and rhythm of the song.

Amanda could not believe how good Keith was at pleasing her orally. Keith could not believe how natural and aesthetically pleasing her *universe* tasted to him. She was already on the verge of *peaking* but was trying her best not to climax too fast. Amanda was moaning earlier but when Keith's warm tongue began to lick circles on her swollen clit, she grabbed and squeeze the thousand count bed sheets with both of her hands. Keith felt her breathing heavier and smirked quietly because he knew he hadn't even got into his *rhythm* with his tongue yet.

With his wet and warm tongue, he licked the right side of her clit then switched to the other side. Then he s-l-o-w-l-y licked up the middle. It was a good thing that Keith placed that towel under her. Her liquid *feminine heat* began flowing all over the place. Keith then licked his right middle and ring fingers then slowly inserted them into her wet pussy. He leaned forward and put her throbbing clit in his mouth. He raised his head slowly and gently licked it in small circles clockwise while sliding his fingers in and out and up against her G-spot. Amanda's back quickly arched with every erotic stroke from his tongue. As his rhythm increased, so did her heart rate and breathing. Feeling the intensity of her nerve-endings increase with sensitivity, she quietly yelled, "...mmhmm, damn...ooooh shit! What the fuck Keith!?" With a wolfish grin, Keith continued with the oral conversation with her Garden of Eden.

She removed one of her hands from squeezing the sheets and placed it on top of Keith's head silently praying he wouldn't stop this moment of ecstasy. He telepathically heard her silent request. Keith kept the rhythm of doing small circular motions with his tongue and fingering her G-spot.

Keith loved being in charge when it came to pleasing his woman. So he gave her clit one last lick from the tip of her clit all-the-way-down to her asshole. Then Keith spread her legs wide and tilted *his head to the side* and slowly slid his *entire* tongue in and out of her universe. He really wanted to taste ALL of her. Keith raised her left leg and placed it over his right shoulder while continuing to stimulate her clit with his fingers. Amanda gasped in ecstasy! She was fighting her climax but now it was definitely getting closer since this frat-boy was in control.

He continued sliding his tongue in and out of her universe in a fast motion while doing circles on her clit with his wet fingertip. He then put his tongue back on her clit and started licking it side to side (left to right) fast like an energizer bunny while stroking her pussy with two fingers. Amanda began *rotating* her hips to the stroke of Keith's tongue.

After about one to two minutes, Amanda could no longer hold in her climax. She was filled with new feelings and enlightenment within her feminine world. She squeezed the bed sheets with one hand, arched her back, and threw her head back against the pillow. His oral pleasures took her up, up, up, and over into exotic waves of unending ecstasy. Her feminine muscles clinched around his fingers… she held her breath and violently *released* her *liquid heat* all over his fingers and tongue. By this time, Amanda was half twisted in the bed with her hand still resting on the top of Keith's head as if her hand was glued to it.

After a moment of hyperventilating and mini convulsions, she finally gained her composure by repositioning herself on her back. After removing the hair that was resting her face, she looked down at Keith as though he was a God. He had a devilish smirk on his face as if he were a surgeon completing a heart transplant. She then motioned Keith to move forward towards her face. Even though Keith had her *universal rain* all over his lips, she leaned forward and kissed him passionately. The way she was kissing him was as if her anticipation of that moment was everything she had dreamed it would be. Their tongues twisting and turning together, fully consuming each other. As she kissed him, she reached down and unbuckled his belt and unbuttoned his pants. She reached below his waist and felt his enlarged member. When Amanda reached to grab his manhood, she rolled her eyes in the back of her head at the size of his cock. "Thank-you—Jesus", she silently said to herself as she stroked Keith's *manhood* up and down with her hand.

She stroked his endowed cock faster and begged Keith to put *him* inside her. Keith reached into his pocket and pulled out a condom. He took his time opening the gold wrapper as if to play with her because he knew how bad she wanted to feel him inside her. While Keith took his time unwrapping the condom, Amanda took the liberty to grab his cock and lick the head of it. She started sucking it slowly to extend his erection. After putting on the condom, Keith began to kiss her again. He was hard as

SEDUCTION

rock and was ready to let Amanda know what he was working with. He whispered in her ear, "put it in for me". She quickly did as commanded.

While laying on her back, once the head of his dick met the opening of her pussy, Amanda crossed her legs behind Keith's back to let him know that she was all his. Keith slowly slid in….. Amanda breathed in deeply to take all of him. Keith began stroking her deep and slow. Then his rhythm increased as he stroked her faster while pulling her hair back by reach behind her back. Still kissing her on her neck, he kept that slow and deep rhythm. Amanda complimented his work by staying wet for him. He was stroking Amanda slightly rough, but passionately. She closed her eyes and intense sensations took over. She felt his girth that complimented his thick and hardness that was joining her feminine universe. She instinctively bent her legs to keep him inside her allowing his enlarged member to glide in and out of her.

Amanda wrapped her legs around his waist, pushing her hips into him, so that each consecutive thrust allowed him to more depth within her. "Right there, please… please don't stop" she begged him. Keith kept it steady resulting in Amanda embedding her nails into Keith's back. Somewhere between fantasy and reality, she *peaked* for the second time… again her feminine muscles *clinched* around his manhood. After a momentary pause for Amanda to catch her breath, Keith then flipped her over on her belly.

He had promise to *aim to please* and he was going to be a man of his word. When she rolled over onto her belly, he glided back inside her warm moist universe and *owned* her secret garden by stroking it faster and deeper. After about five minutes in that position, he gritted his teeth together and released with a powerful moan and then slowly laid himself next to her.

They both laid there motionless for a few minutes while Trey Songz "Jupiter Love" played quietly in the background. Amanda had worked twelve hours at the hospital and had climaxed twice. She was *done!* She leaned over to kiss Keith then smiled and said "Thank you… I needed that!" as her head collapsed back onto the pillow. Then she slowly slid out of the bed and walked towards the bathroom to freshen up a bit. Keith laid there and shook his head at the thought of the passionate love that they just exchanged.

After a small bathroom visit, they finally ate the breakfast that Keith had brought for them. They kept looking at each other while eating with smirks on their faces. Amanda could not remember the last time she was pleased the way Keith had pleased her. She tried her best to entertain Keith but she had climaxed twice and her body couldn't take it. She was falling asleep right in front of him. Drooling and everything! Keith picked up Amanda and walked her upstairs. He laid her onto her bed. He knew she had to work that night so he tucked her in bed. Amanda curled up like a baby ready for bed. "You can stay if you want too…" was her last words to Keith as she fell asleep.

Keith reached over and set her alarm clock two hours before she normally had to go to work. Keith kissed her on her forehead, got fully dressed and grabbed his things. He started to stay with her for a while but decided to wait. He quietly walked downstairs and locked the door as he left.

5

THE EX FACTOR

Keith and Amanda had shared their first intimate experience that God himself seemed to had shined his light on. Keith was beginning to feel that Amanda was *the one*. If she wasn't the one, then he felt literally caught up in some sort of matrix of love or lust. Keith was the kinda brother who was getting his way with the ladies for years. No real commitments, just dating. However, Amanda was beginning to turn the table on his player lifestyle.

After the first experience of intimacy, the two would have "breakfast and chill" as often as they could while being discreet about their secret relationship at work. Keith started talking less and less to the female friends he that was in his phone and on social media. At this point, Amanda was starting to have his full attention. She was also getting very attached to Keith. She knew he was a flirt, but she also knew that he was falling for her. Sometimes she overheard other nurses on the floor talking about Keith and their attractiveness for him not knowing that she was secretly sleeping with him. Just to be sure that she wasn't getting played, she asked Keith about the females he was friends with before her. He told her that he was no longer interested in them anymore since they were getting closer. He sarcastically answered and said, "as long as you *act* right, it'll stay that way." She just laughed and said "Whatever Keith, don't let me find out!"

One morning after they had eaten breakfast at Amanda's apartment, the two were about to make love but it was interrupted by Amanda's cell as it kept ringing. She looked at the contact name on the screen of her phone and answered it slowly with a stunned look on her face. Then she got up from the couch and looked at her front door as if someone was standing outside of it. She walked towards the door and gently opened it. She looked a Keith and told him that she would be right back then walked out of the door.

Keith was a bit puzzled. He walked toward the front window of the living room and peeped through the blinds to see who it was that called her. Obviously, it must have been important if she hopped off the couch like that, thought Keith. He opened the blind wide enough to see

Amanda walk towards a gray Ford F150 with chrome wheels and low profile tires. Even though the windows on the truck were lightly tinted, Keith could see that there was a dark skinned guy in the driver's seat. Keith decided to play it cool. He didn't want to jump to any crazy conclusions because in reality, it could have been a relative of hers. But then again, he remembered Amanda mentioned that most, if not all, of her family lived in Georgia.

Keith continued to watch through the blinds and noticed that the guy never got out of the truck but seemed to be fussing with Amanda. Then the guy reached over and handed Amanda a huge black trash bag that was filled with her belongings. Then it dawned on Keith, it was Amanda's ex-boyfriend!

Keith started thinking to himself, maybe the chapter wasn't closed in their relationship like Amanda had initially told him. Keith started thinking that maybe he came into her life at the wrong time while they were just separated. While these thoughts ran through his mind, Keith heard the truck change gears as if switching into drive to leave. As they (Amanda and her ex) exchanged last words, Keith saw the expression in Amanda's demeanor that suggested that this was the final closure between the two… if that was her ex-boyfriend.

The truck slowly left the parking lot and Amanda walked back towards her apartment. Keith rushed back onto the couch as though he was sitting there the entire time. She walked into the apartment and sat the black bag full of her things on the floor. When the bag hit the floor, one heel fell out of the bag onto the floor along with a small stuffed green turtle. It was indeed the remainder of her things that she had at her ex's place.

Keith didn't want to start an argument without the facts, but he wanted to be sure it was her ex. So, he asked her who that was in the truck. She said that it was her ex, Steven. Then she turned away as she shut the door, locked it and walked quietly upstairs. Amanda felt so embarrassed at what just happened mainly because it happened while Keith was there. She didn't mention any more about it to Keith that day.

6

ROUND 2

Weeks passed and every so often Keith discovered incoming text messages on Amanda's phone from her ex Steven. Apparently, Steven was missing Amanda and wanted her back in his life again. The texts continued until it got to the point of Keith arguing with Amanda for still being in touch with her ex. Keith had stopped texting his ex, jump-offs, and even potential encounters prior to them becoming serious and didn't think it was right for her to still text Steven. However, Amanda assured Keith that she was over her ex and was ready to move on with him.

As time passed, Keith continued to visit Amanda after or before work. They both wanted to see each other more often. They were getting closer and still *fooling around*. If anything, the lovemaking sessions *were* becoming more frequent and more intense. They even got to the point where they were making love like rabbits everywhere throughout Amanda's apartment.

※

One day while making love, the intimacy was interrupted by the sound of the doorbell. Keith said to Amanda, "that bet not be that motherfucker (her ex) again!" Amanda looked out her bedroom window, which was upstairs, it was just the Orkin man. She got dressed and walked downstairs to let him in so he could do the quarterly pesticide treatment. Meanwhile, Keith was upstairs holding his hard manhood in his hand.

Amanda greeted the exterminator and told him that she would be upstairs for a few minutes and that if he needed anything just to let her know. Apparently, Amanda was very familiar with him. The exterminator started spraying treatment downstairs beginning with the living room and kitchen. Meanwhile, the song *"that's what it's made for"* by Usher was still playing in the background and the two were still horny!

Keith grabbed Amanda's hand, took her into the guest room, and partially closed the door. Keith knew the *spots* on Amanda's body that made her horny when kissed or touched. He knew exactly where to kiss her to get her wet. He laid her down on the guest bed and began his sensual assault. He began kissing her all over those intimate *spots*.

Amanda was hesitant to participate at first. She said to him, "Keith, I go to church with that old man... this is wrong!" He pretended not to hear her and started going *downtown* on her anyway. Keith knew he had at least a few minutes to play before the exterminator would make his way upstairs. It didn't take Keith long to get Amanda to the climax zone. He was sliding his fingers in and out of her pussy while stimulating her clit with his tongue. She was on the verge of peaking. Then he stopped licking her clit. *Why stop now, I am nervous about us getting caught and was just about to climax,* said Amanda silently! Amanda's heart was pounding and her adrenaline was spiked through her body at the possibility of peaking and them getting caught being intimate.

※

Keith rotated Amanda her on her left side and got behind her (spooning position) while under the blanket. He grabbed Amanda's small waist and started stroking her deep and slow. "We shouldn't be doing this Keith!" She whispered to Keith while moaning with each stroke he gave her. They heard the exterminator walking up the stairs but Keith didn't stop, he kept his rhythm.

The exterminator then entered the upstairs bathroom and then into her bedroom. Next, he came to the guest room door where they were still grinding and said, "...do you want me to spray in here too mam?" They didn't even

SEDUCTION

look or answered the poor old man. The old man peek inside and saw Keith's hips moving forwards and backwards under the blanket. The exterminator said, "Y'all have a good day!" then hurried down the stairs and left the apartment. That's how much of a freak they were to each other.

7

POWER TRIP

Keith and Amanda became exclusive partners. Everyone at work now knew of their relationship. However, weeks passed and the text messages and phone calls from her ex began interrupting their new relationship. After a few weeks of the periodic messages, Keith became fed up with the situation. *If her ex was still texting her that meant Amanda was still replying,* Keith thought. Keith was tired of it and he ended their relationship. They broke up for nearly two months. During that time, Keith did his best to avoid Amanda while working at Wake Med North. Sometimes he wouldn't even do security checks on Amanda's floor just so he wouldn't see her.

One night Keith even gave her a parking ticket for parking in a patient's parking space. The next morning when Amanda saw the ticket on her windshield, she automatically knew it was Keith! She walked to her car and snatched the ticket from her windshield. She angrily marched straight to the security office looking upset as hell. Keith knew she would come to the office after she saw the ticket so he made sure not to be in there when she got off work that morning. The only officer in the office was Keith's supervisor Sgt. Anderson. He was sitting at his desk completing a report and eating breakfast. One thing you could count on with Sgt. Anderson; either he is eating or sleeping in the office when no one was in there.

She walked into the office and yelled, "Where is he?" while looking around the office simultaneously! "Who Keith? He left about five minutes ago. I'm sure he will be back soon though. Why? What's wrong?" "He gave me damn a ticket!" she yelled. "Look Amanda, whatever's going on between you two, y'all need to take that crap somewhere else! Let me hold the ticket... I'll get rid of it!" said his supervisor. Their breakup was ugly!

During their breakup, Amanda decided to get away for a week by going home to Georgia to visit family. A hurricane had recently came through there. Fortunately, her family and the town were not affected by the storm. While Amanda was in Georgia with her family, Keith was still in Raleigh doing his thing. The same weekend Amanda left to go home to Georgia, Keith went to a city outside of Durham to hang out with some of his fraternity brothers.

That night they all went out to eat at a Caribbean restaurant. Afterwards, they went to one of his frat's apartment to watch a basketball game. They were just relaxing and practicing the latest party-hops (fraternity dance moves) with their canes. Keith was in the middle of talking to one of his frat brothers while twirling his cane when his cell phone rang. It was Amanda.

Keith looked at his phone and started not to answer it. Since he hadn't heard her voice in a while, he decided to answer the phone. He acted nonchalantly as if he didn't want to talk to her.

He answered with a low deep voice, "Yeah… what's up?"

Amanda who almost melted at the sound of hearing Keith's deep voice said, "Nothing, at my mom's house. What are you up to?"

"I'm at my frat's house just twirling my cane and practicing some new moves." said Keith.

"…yeah, whatever!", Amanda said in a spunky sarcastic tone.

That tone of voice was too familiar to Keith. He knew what that *type* of tone meant; she missed him! They talked briefly on the phone then said their goodbyes. From the tone of their conversation, they both knew that as soon as

SEDUCTION

she got back in from Georgia, they would be back together again.

"Damn frat, she got you all smiling and shit! Thought y'all broke up." said one of his frats. "We did bruh, but I can tell she miss this *cane* and that *rabbit!*" said Keith with a serious face while holding his crouch and licking his tongue up and down between his two fingers. They all burst out laughing at Keith!

8

RIGHT THING WRONG REASONS

As anticipated, when Amanda got back from Georgia, they got it on! They were like rabbits again. For weeks, they were becoming more intimate everywhere in Amanda's apartment. They were getting it on like they never broke up. Every morning, every evening, after work and before going to work was spent making love. They would make love three-times-a-day some days.

One day as fate would hate it, Amanda realized that her period was late. She was NEVER late. She told Keith about her period being late but her news didn't surprise him. As much as they were getting it on, pregnancy was certainly a possibility. The next morning after getting off work, Amanda stopped by the closest pharmacy store near her apartment. While in the store, Amanda ran into another nurse who worked on the same floor with her at

Wake Med. This coworker was a bit older than Amanda. Even though Maria was almost forty years old, she looked like she could be in her mid-twenties. She was very young at heart. She was from Miami and was a true Latina with her beauty and bluntness of speech! Amanda did her best to hide the pregnancy test from her co-worker but Maria saw it anyway.

"Mami, who do you think you're fooling? We were all already thinking that you were pregnant by the way you've been throwing up all over the place. You and Papi been gett'n your groove on, aye, what do you think?" asked Maria who didn't know how to whisper. "Child, I don't even know. I just know I'm late and I'm never late! I'm so nervous! I'll let you know if I am though!", replied Amanda. "Listen Mami, don't worry, everything will be okay! You will make a great mother! Be sure to let me know, I work tonight too!" said Maria. They hugged each other and Maria left. Amanda paid for the pregnancy test and left the store feeling somewhat at ease from Maria's words.

The drive from the pharmacy to her apartment seemed like the longest ride for Amanda. She started crying before she even got home at the possibility of her being pregnant. When she made it home, she walked inside, dropped her things on the floor and went straight upstairs to start the test. Sure enough, she was *pregnant*.

Amanda took a deep breath and started crying! Considering that she had just got out of a five-year relationship with her ex, she wasn't quite sure how to react to the pregnancy test. She had really loved Steven, but was now in love with Keith. "Should I keep it or get it aborted? How will I explain this to Steven (her ex) since we have only been broken up less than a year? Am I even ready to be a mother? Will I be a single mom? Will Keith leave me after I tell him the news?" Those were just *some* of the many questions running through Amanda's mind.

That same night, Amanda texted Keith's phone and asked for him to call her whenever he was free. As soon as Keith received the text, he had a feeling it had to do with Amanda's pregnancy test. She had already told him that she was going to stop by the pharmacy to get the test earlier that day. Keith had been anxious the entire day. He didn't eat or sleep well all day! Even the drive to work was stressful for him. Keith was stopped by a police officer for speeding. Keith never sped to get anyway but he was speeding while caught up in thought of the possibility of Amanda being pregnant. Since, it was a very slow night at work for Keith, he decided to call her right then and there.

Phone rings:

"Hello…" said Amanda.
"Hey…" replied Keith.

P-A-U-S-E

"Did you get a chance to stop by the..." but before Keith could finish, Amanda interrupted, "yeah, I did...(sigh)... and I'm pregnant Keith!"

"Are you sure?" asked Keith rhetorically.

Amanda said, "ahh—yeah, I took two tests just to be sure."

"Oooh okay... I just wanted to make sure that's all.... I mean, I just needed to ask...I guess we need to... I mean I guess I should... wow okay, I mean.... Wow, I'm excited about the news baby!" said Keith.

Amanda wasn't sure how Keith would react to the news. Emotionally, she went from feeling sad and crying to laughing at Keith's stuttering! Although she loved Keith, she was a bit nervous and scared that he would possibly get mad or walk away at the news.

For the rest of the night, Keith was a mixture of happy and nervous! He was about to be a father for the first time in his life. "Am I ready for this? Can I be as good as a father that my father was to me? What will my parents think of me having a child out-of-wedlock?" Were some of the questions Keith had running laps around in his mind all night while at work! He was about to be a father!

A few days later, Amanda called and made an appointment with an OBGYN doctor. Keith made sure he was there to accompany her to the doctor's office. They discovered that Amanda was about seven weeks pregnant. Being a product of church going parents who were still married, Keith wanted to do the right thing and mirror the philosophy of his upbringing about having a child. Moreover, he really loved Amanda. After about a month after the news of her pregnancy, Keith pondered the idea of asking Amanda to marry him.

One evening, they had a nice dinner and decided to return to Amanda's apartment to enjoy Netflix. After the movie ended, Amanda wanted some strawberry ice cream from downstairs. When Keith returned to Amanda, he totally surprised her! Not only did he brought her favorite ice cream but he got down on one knee and proposed to her! It wasn't a fashion statement with his proposal, but Keith wanted to let Amanda know how much he really loved her. Without hesitation, Amanda said yes to his proposal! She was excited to know that Keith was serious about commitment! They were officially engaged to be married. Amanda took a deep breath while looking at her new engagement ring. She was excited but in the back of her mind, Amanda wanted to make sure Keith wasn't proposing just because she was pregnant.

One evening, Amanda called Keith and asked him to meet her in a local supermarket parking lot. When Keith arrived, he parked beside her car and motioned her to come sit in his car. Amanda slowly got out, walked over towards Keith, and sat in his car. Amanda had some major concerns about her pregnancy and wanted to ask Keith a question that was hunting her since the proposal.

Amanda was full of emotions. Before she could get her first few words out, she started crying! Keith knew she was emotional due to the hormonal change with the pregnancy but felt that there was something more to Amanda's crying. She couldn't hold it in any longer... she said, "Keith, you know I love you baby and I know you love me. But I just want to make sure you didn't propose to me just because I'm pregnant...did you?"

"What? Amanda I..." said Keith before he was interrupted by Amanda again.

"Keith shut up!!! Please... just listen, please! I just wanna make sure we are getting married for the *right reasons* and not just because I'm pregnant! We don't have to get married right now. I don't want you to marry me for the wrong reason!" cried Amanda.

Keith with confidence said "No, I want-to-marry-you. It's not because you're pregnant! Amanda, I love you baby!"

Amanda seemed relieved by Keith's confident reply to her questions and concerns. She didn't really know how he would respond but she was glad he responded the way he did. She wanted to be married as well but had always imagined being married before having a child. Amanda dried her tears, reached over, and gave Keith a hug. In the back of Keith's mind, he was thinking the same thing. He really loved Amanda but was also trying to do the right thing as a man. He wanted to do the right thing as a father. To accept responsibility for his seed because he was always taught that if you're going to have children you should be married. He wanted to live up to those expectations.

9

JOY AND PAIN

A few months later, great things started to happen for the new couple. Keith moved in with Amanda in her apartment for a few weeks and then they moved into their new home. Their first home together. A lot of transitions were happening. Keith left his job as a security officer at Wake Med North and was hired as a police officer for the city of Raleigh. Everything seemed to be going just perfect for them. They were living in a new home, about to be married, and have a child. The nurse was about to marry a future police officer. Five months into the pregnancy, they found out great news. They were expecting a baby boy. Keith was so excited to have a son as his first child! He could barely contain it!

Keith was accepted to go to the police academy to work for the city of Raleigh when Amanda was almost five months pregnant. The academy was thirteen weeks long.

Amanda and Keith agreed that he should attend the academy considering the fact that he should be graduating the academy before she would be due to have the baby. Keith thought to himself of all the wonderful things that were happening for him and his new family! Everything seemed to be falling in place and going according to plan! He then thought to himself that this all is just too good to be true!

Keith started training at the academy and entered his first week. It was *do or die* time for him. He had so much on the line. He would have to pass every exam every Friday in order to stay in the academy. However, as fate would have it, Amanda began to contractions that caused serious complications and a premature birth of their son during his first week in the academy.

Amanda was rushed to the hospital for complications. Her mother had driven up from Georgia a few days earlier to be a help to her while Keith was away at training. It was Thursday evening when Amanda's mom called Keith to let him know about Amanda being rushed to the hospital because to the complications. She told him that the doctors were able to suspend the delivery temporarily. Keith began to gather his things while he was on the phone with her mom. Hearing Keith becoming worried, Amanda's mom stopped him. She had told him that the delivery was suspended and that Amanda wanted him to stay at the academy to focus on the exam that he needed to pass the next day.

Her mom promised Keith that she would call him back if Amanda's status changed. Since the academy was only ten to fifteen minutes away from Wake Med, it worked out. At that time, Amanda was about five foot one, maybe a hundred and fifteen pounds soaking wet while pregnant and that made the delivery that much more complicated.

A few hours passed. Around 4:45 am the following morning, Keith received a phone call from Amanda's mother. Amanda had delivered the baby. The labor pain had hit Amanda and before she knew it, the baby was delivered. Even though the baby was born nearly three months premature, fortunately the baby boy would be okay.

When Keith heard the good news, he immediately jumped up out of his bed and got dressed. He hopped into his SS Camaro and sped towards the hospital. When he arrived at Wake Med, he was a bit upset that he had missed the delivery but was thankful that Amanda and their first born were fine! Since the initial phone call, Keith was stressed thinking of it all. What if something goes wrong with the delivery? What if the baby stops breathing or Amanda died during the delivery? Those were some of the racing thoughts Keith had in his head after Amanda's mother spoke with him earlier.

Keith arrived at the bedside of Amanda. She was still a bit sore and exhausted from the delivery. She was now resting. When she saw Keith, she started crying at the joy on Keith's face. "He's here baby. He has a loud mouth and has your egg-head too…" whispered Amanda while smiling. Keith let out a small laugh while the tears flowed and replied, "Yeah, he probably does…" He leaned forward, kissed Amanda on her forehead and whispered in her ear how much he loved her!

Since the baby was born premature by almost three months, he had to be sent to the NICU for more observation to ensure he was healthy enough to go home.

Keith was officially a father! "If you want to see him, he is in the neonatal intensive care unit. They have to observe him for a while! But Keith, after you see him, please go back to the academy and finish up your exam. I know how important this is for you! We will be fine here until you get back. You'll have plenty of time to be with us after you get finished with your exam. We will be okay baby… now go see him and get back there!" Said Amanda.

Keith was both inspired and impressed with Amanda's fortitude. He did as she requested. He gave Amanda a gentle kiss on her lips and then gave her mother a hug. He took last look at Amanda, smiled, and exited the hospital room. He made his way to the Neonatal Intensive Care Unit(NICU). Keith was so nervous about seeing his son for the first time! He was dressed in his academy uniform so everyone seemed to notice him as he entered the NICU and approached the nurse's station.

After showing his identification, Keith was escorted by a young vibrant Caucasian nurse to see his son. When Keith arrived to the area where his son was sleeping, he laid eyes on his son for the first time. He looked angelic and precious to Keith. Because he was in an incubator, Keith was only able to reach through the opening with his forearms and hands to hold him. His baby boy only weighed two pounds eight ounces. He literally was the size of Keith's hand. Keith held him for a few minutes then laid him down so the baby could get some rest.

When the nurse saw how emotional Keith was becoming while holding his son, she walked over and opened the top of the incubator. She allowed Keith to take his son out briefly to kiss him on the forehead. Keith tried not to cry but tears flowed down his cheeks when he laid eyes on his son! Keith and Amanda had decided to name their baby boy after Keith…Keith Jacob James Jr. Keith sat and just stared at his son for as long as he could. He does have an egghead like me, he thought to himself as he smiled at baby boy Keith Jr.

Keith thanked the nurse who escorted him to see his son, then left the hospital to return to the academy to take the exam. He was more excited than ever to see Keith Jr again. His goal was to get back in time to take the exam, pass it, and immediately go back to his family.

Keith packed so many different emotions with him and took them into the classroom. Before he knew it, it was already time to take the exam. This was the first exam for the academy. The exam wasn't supposed to be too hard for the officer candidates. The instructor walked around the classroom and handed out the exams. When Keith received the exam and laid eyes on it, his mind went completely blank! He had studied some throughout the week, well at least tried to study, and felt prepared.

He started the exam anyway. He struggled a bit but managed to finish the exam. He even finished early. While waiting for the other candidates to finish taking their exam, Keith waited outside the classroom with some of his classmates.

Keith began to share with them his excitement of his new son KJ (Keith Jr). They were giving him high-fives and hugs to congratulate him! After about thirty minutes of waiting outside, the rest of the students were all finally done taking the exam. Keith waited for the results of the exam. All he needed was to see his name on the list and his passing score so he could get back to seeing his wife and son. A few minutes later, the results were posted on the classroom door. Everyone rushed to get their passing score. Keith pushed through the dense crowd and reached with his finger to find his name. He finally found his name Keith James and slid his finger over to the right to find his grade. He failed the exam! Keith failed the exam by one question. He needed a 70% to continue on to next week of training but he made a failing score of 68%.

10

SILENT FRUSTRATION

That Friday was the best of times and the worst of times for Keith. He was so joyful just a few hours prior because of the birth of his first son and just that quick, it all went sour. Keith knew if he failed that exam, his department had the option to terminate him. Keith, was so embarrassed but knew he had to call his department to let them know that he failed the exam. After he made the call, they told him that he had to immediately report back to the police station. When he got there, they were highly disappointed in Keith. However, after Keith explained to them what happened, they quickly understood his situation and decided to give him another opportunity. They explained to him that he would need to wait a few weeks to return to the academy.

Keith left the station and went home. He changed his clothes and decided to drive Amanda's car. Since it was a

SEDUCTION

four-door sedan, it would be more comfortable for her to ride back home in. Being both upset and embarrassed, Keith began the drive to the hospital.

When he arrived at the hospital, Amanda took one look at Keith's face and knew something was wrong. She saw the look on Keith's face and immediately knew he had failed the exam. He told her what happened. To his surprise, Amanda was very supportive. She said, "Don't worry about it baby, we will be alright. I know it was a lot to have on your mind while testing, but we will be fine." That was exactly what Keith needed to hear at that moment. Two days later Amanda was discharged to go home.

After about two months, Keith's department decided to give him another chance at being a police officer. Keith was beyond excited. He was more focused than ever! He assured them that he was more than ready to return to the academy. When Keith returned, he excelled with the exams and training. It was a piece of cake now. The hardest exams were done. All that was left were minor exams and maybe three weeks remaining at the training site.

Because KJ was a *"preme"*, he had to stay as a patient in the hospital until he reached healthy weight. Keith and Amanda had set their original date to be married during this time. Even though KJ was still a patient, they decided to go ahead and follow through with it. They decided to get married during a weekend at their new home just outside of Raleigh. The week leading up to the wedding, the two were excited and had beautiful conversations by phone since Keith was still at the academy.

Nevertheless, the day before the wedding, Keith and Amanda had a huge argument. Keith was moving things around inside the house preparing for the wedding when he discovered a photo of her ex that was hidden in of one of her dresser-drawers under her underwear. That was the last place Amanda thought Keith would look for anything. It was a 4 X 4 picture of her ex-boyfriend holding his dick in his hand.

Naturally, Keith became furious! He couldn't believe she was holding onto anything belonging to her ex, let alone a picture like that one! He was upset because that was something that she should have gotten rid of after they became engaged or when they became serious!

While confronting Amanda, their argument became louder and louder within the house! Amanda's mother, who was sitting in the living room interrupted the loud argument. Amanda's mother was very quiet most times. She was about five foot nine and roughly two hundred and seventy-five pounds. Big-Boned. However, this time she stood to her feet, raised her voice and said, "I need you two to hear me and hear me well! If you guys can't get over it or if either one of you know that you haven't finished a chapter in your life, then it's best for y'all not to get married. Because you need to close it before moving on and getting married."

Even though she said those words, they decided to go ahead and get married anyway. Keith really loved Amanda and their newborn. He figured that things would have to change once they became married. The wedding was held the next day. They said their vows and were pronounced Mr. and Mrs. James. Everything was supposed to go smooth and they planned to live happily ever after. Even though that was their plan, *things* started happening that some people would call a *clue*. As if finding the picture of her ex's dick before the wedding wasn't already a clue… that would only be a forewarning of things that would come up again in the future.

A few days after the wedding, their son Keith Jr was finally released to go home. KJ had been a patient in the hospital for nearly three months and had significant gained the weight needed for discharge. Because of special health conditions from being a premature baby, KJ needed to be placed on a special heart and oxygen monitor for at least a month after being released from the hospital. Keith and Amanda had to stay with him the night before the release to make sure they were able to work the monitors. Keith was still in the police academy. It's now the final week and he was about to take one of the easiest exams in the academy. Considering that Keith knew the material well, he decided to go to the hospital and stay with Amanda at the hospital.

Keith brought his textbook with him to study while there. He figured he would study the material when KJ went to sleep. Keith had anticipated KJ going to sleep around 8 or 9 p.m. that night. He and Amanda felt that KJ would sleep all night. That night KJ stayed awake all-night-long. KJ cried for what seem like the entire night. Not only did Keith not study as he planned, but he didn't sleep either.

When morning came, KJ finally went to sleep. Keith kissed him and Amanda who was slightly awake then left to head back to the academy. While on the way, he stopped by the closest gas station to get some coffee before getting to class. This was the easiest exam so Keith didn't seem too worried by the lack of sleep or studying for this one. It's test time! It was the same process as the rest of the exams. Everyone had to wait until all the candidates were finished with their exam before a candidate could find out their exam score.

After forty-five minutes, the candidates were all finished. The exam scores were posted on the classroom door. Keith found his name as he had the past few weeks. He had passed all the other tests with flying colors and knew exactly where to find his name. Keith failed the exam! Not only did he fail the easiest exam, but he failed by only one question... again! Keith was crushed. It felt like de ja' vu all over again. After speaking with the training staff at the academy, he had to go pack his belongings like last time and notify his department. Keith's classmates felt awful for Keith. They were cheering for him being a new father and this happened. Keith wanted to cry but held it back as much as he could while in their presence. He had to make the same phone call to his department to let them know that he had failed.

This was the second time Keith failed. He knew that after the second failure he would no longer have a job at the police department. The academy's rule was only two failures per year. Keith was so baffled. He had just got married, had a child, but no longer had a job to support his family. Keith felt deep down inside that maybe God had a different plan for him. Maybe it wasn't meant for him to be a police officer anyway. He felt like maybe it's the wrong timing or something.

After traveling back to the police department, Keith met with his department and turned in his uniforms. He drove back to the hospital and had to explain his embarrassment to Amanda. She was up and vibrant while holding KJ. After confessing the awful news to her, Amanda surprisingly didn't fuss at him again. She wasn't even upset with him. She knew that he didn't get any sleep the night before the exam. Amanda felt terrible about Keith failing. She knew how much he wanted to pass the exam. She wished she had let him sleep or at least study for the exam. She leaned over, kissed Keith, and said, "Keith, everything is going to be alright baby. Maybe you weren't supposed to be a cop anyway!" and smiled. Keith smiled back but as a man, Keith knew that everything wasn't alright. He had a feeling that everything was not going to be okay. Keith had left home at seventeen to join the military. He was able to sustain himself ever since. He knew that he had to do something and do something fast! He was a married man and a father…he had to do something.

The next month, Keith decided to apply for nursing school. He had served on active duty in the military for four years as a medic, so he felt pretty confident that he could make it through nursing school. He could use the G.I. Bill and would get paid through the benefits. That would be additional financial help for his family. He applied for nursing school at Wake Technical College and was accepted.

Keith was excited again! It felt good to know that he was on his way to doing something positive for his family. Trying to balance a new life, a marriage, a new home life and being a father for the first time wasn't easy for Keith. Amanda was back to work as a nurse and things were beginning to balance out even though he wasn't the breadwinner in the home.

As if failing the academy wasn't enough, Keith failed the first semester of nursing school by half a point. Keith was like "half a damn point? How the hell did I fail this shit by half a damn point?" But since he had steady income coming from the G.I. Bill, Keith decided to stay in school. He knew that he needed to take more classes to keep the benefits active. He loaded his class schedule with as many classes that it took to keep him busy for the next two semesters. Keith became an academic hustler!

About a year later, Keith contemplated the idea of become a police officer again. He thought it would be a great idea. He was no longer in nursing school. His thought was that he could work full-time as an officer and take a few classes at night or online. His home life was more stable and he felt that he was able to concentrate if given the opportunity to go back to the academy. He could go back to the academy and take his classes online. So he went back to the city of Raleigh to see if they would hire him back. Unfortunately, they denied Keith the opportunity to come back to work for them. Their decision bothered the hell out of Keith. He was never late for work or anything. His uniform was always sharp and he got along with everyone when he worked there. Keith became very frustrated, but he decided to use their denial as motivation for his next goal.

11

OLD FLAME

About a year later

One evening after working long hours, it was time for Amanda to go home for the day after working a busy day. She called home to let Keith know that she was leaving work and was now on her way home. She was excited to get off work at a decent hour so she could have extra time to be with her family. Keith had already had dinner prepared so she didn't even have to cook, so she was more than excited for that! After she hung up the phone with Keith, she pulled up to an intersection that was about ten minutes away from her home. While stopped at the traffic light, her favorite gospel song was on the radio. She was very tired from being on her feet all day but was never too tired to sing along with her gospel music.

While waiting at the traffic light, a silver Ford truck pulled up next to her in the traffic lane to her left. She briefly looked over at the truck then looked back at the red light while singing the gospel song that was playing on the radio. The truck looked somewhat familiar to her but she didn't pay any attention to it. The driver of the truck slowly rolled down the tinted passenger's side window... and... it was Steven, Amanda's ex! He saw her while passing and decided to make a U-turn to follow her. He sped up then maneuvered in and out of traffic but finally caught up with her.

While his window was rolled down, he nonchalantly looked over to his right towards her direction and blew his horn. He was wearing a white tank top, a Chicago Bulls hat (backwards), while wearing dark shades and smoking a Churchill style cigar. Amanda looked over to the left in the direction of the horn. They caught eye contact. The first time in almost two years. She couldn't believe it, it was Steven! He gangsterly nodded at her and smiled. She looked in his direction then quickly turned away with her eyes crinkling at the corners. She tried so hard not to smile back at him. Seeing him reminded her of their wonderful but fractured memories. Amanda's palms began to sweat while gripping the steering wheel tighter with each passing second. The red light seemed to be the longest red light she had ever had to stop for. Seeing that Amanda was tensing up behind the steering wheel, Steven then blew the horn again. By this time, an incoming call from Keith came across her cell phone. Amanda never ignored Keith's phone calls before...*but this time she did.* She turned from the direction of her cell phone and looked back at Steven. He smiled then waved at her. Amanda was very reluctant but smiled and waved back at him. Amanda then quickly turned and looked straight ahead and began talking to herself. *"What the HELL are you doing Amanda? It's OVER between you and Steven"*, she silently prayed.

She looked back at her ex Steven, smiled one more time, then sped off by making a right turn towards her home. Her ex saw that she was alone while she was at the light so he decided to text her.

"You still ugly!"

"Whateva, YOU know better..." she replied immediately.

"I see you all married now and your hubby's busy in school all the time... How is robo-cop doing anyway? You didn't look too happy while at the traffic light. What's wrong?" he wrote.

"I'm good... I mean, we good. Why are you worrying about me anyway? I see you dating someone else. She's my height too. I guess you tried to replace me but there's only one me....remember that!" She replied.

"I really miss you Claire! Been wanting to talk to you since we broke up but I never see you around anymore..." texted her ex.

※

No one called Amanda by her middle name except Steven. After reading the text, she immediately started reminiscing of their time together. After all, they had a five-year history. While thinking about their history of love, she then thought about their nasty breakup! Then she got upset about it all and replied,

"Yeah right! You don't miss me. Why did you wait 'til I get married to tell me?"

"You're still feisty I see... you better get to your hubby before I turn this truck around and come grab you like I use too and..." He said.

"....and? Boy, ain't nobody scared of you. Turn your truck around..." She replied.

Her ex never replied back to her last text. By this time, Amanda had made it all the way across the city and was now pulling up into her driveway. She sat in the car for a few minutes quietly waiting for Steven's reply. She took a long deep breath and rested her head on the car's steering wheel because she hadn't talked nor seen her ex in nearly two years. She was hoping to never see him again, but there he was at the light. "I can't believe that he's *still* here in Raleigh", she thought to herself. She had seen him with another woman on Facebook and Instagram not long after their breakup. As though he found a rebound. Amanda had also noticed that he took all over "their" photos down from social media. A while ago, she had investigated all of his social media pages and scrolled through all his photos in every album just to be sure. She figured he had moved away by now.

To her surprise, he had still looked the same, if not *better*, then when she last saw him. He had lost weight and even put on muscle mass. Amanda, still sitting in the driveway of her home, began to drift off into a daydream about her past relationship with Steven. They had history. She sat in the car reminiscing about their time together, both the good times and the bad. She really thought that she and Steven would have gotten married after college. Each time she thought about the past possibilities of her and Steven, the thought seemed to *seduce* her more and more. Little did Amanda know, she was sitting in the car for over five minutes in a trance.

Amanda, *still* sitting in the driver's seat, sat with her head down and eyes glued to her phone. The way Steven smiled at hear at the traffic light made Amanda hopeful for at least a reply message to her last text. All she wanted was a simple glimpse of what his last thoughts of her was so she could read it, and then quickly erase it before she walked into the house.

By this time, Keith realized that Amanda was home. He had walked past the living room and glanced Amanda's car parked in the driveway. Keith was proud of himself for having dinner ready for his wife who had worked a long day. He felt that it was the least he could do to show his affection for his lovely wife. Keith went into the den, picked up KJ and opened the front door of their home. He walked down the red five level brick stairs while carrying KJ on top of his shoulders. They both were smiling and excited to see Amanda home early from work. Keith walked up to the car and knocked on the window. Amanda jumped in her seat from being startled by both the knock and by Keith's presence. She quickly put her phone down then threw it into her purse and got out of the car. She greeted Keith and KJ with a hug and an innocent kiss! She grabbed her purse and held Keith's hand while walking from the car to the house. Keith thought nothing of the strange way Amanda was acting but discreetly gave her the *side eye* once she got out of her car and while kissing KJ.

After walking into the house, Keith wanted Amanda to hold KJ for a few minutes while he prepared the table for them but Amanda reminded him that she needed to change clothes and shower first. She was always aware of the possibility germs sticking to her uniform from working with patients all day.

Amanda began taking off her uniform. She placed them into the laundry basket, which was in the corner by the shower located in their bathroom. Amanda's heart was now beating fast. She didn't get a chance to erase the text messages! She figured that the more she talked, the more it would distract Keith. She began to pray silently that Steven would NOT text her back while Keith was near her phone or while she was in the shower! The ringer on her phone was still in the *high* position. She quickly hopped into the shower.

While holding KJ, Keith walked into the bedroom and began asked about her day. She went on and on about how busy her day was and how much she loved and missed her family. Amanda talked from the time she got out of her car until she got into the shower. She even talked while in the shower, making sure she was able to engage Keith. After two minutes into the shower, her phone beeped. Amanda was so *busy* talking that she failed to hear the text alert. Keith never really read the text messages in Amanda's phone now that they were married. He decided to give her the benefit of the doubt since they had moved on from the last argument the day of their wedding. Amanda had been a *dedicated* churchgoer and was well known within the community and at her workplace as the model wife and mother. Keith's love and trust was unbroken so far with her.

However, the strange behavior of Amanda now had Keith wondering what was really going on with her that afternoon. Her phone beeped again. Keith figured since Amanda was in the shower he would let her know who texted her. Keith stopped playing with KJ, reached into her purse, and felt around for her phone. He was able to find it while Amanda was steadily talking to him while in the shower. He grabbed her cell phone, lifted it out of the purse, and... it was a *reply* message from her ex.

Steven replied:

> *"My bad! My ol' lady called me after I sent you my last text. But if you wana meet up sometimes to catch up on things...just let me know! I can't wait to see you Claire!"*

By this time, Amanda realized that Keith was quiet and not responding to her. She immediately started panicking. She quickly stuck her head out of the shower and immediately caught eye contact with Keith.

By this time, Keith had read the *entire* conversation between her and Steven. He nonchalantly handed Amanda the phone. Her heart began to pound through her skin. She had no idea how Keith would react to the forbidden conversation. *After all, it was only text messages. It wasn't like she said she wanted to sleep with him,* she thought to herself while stepping out of the shower. Keith pretended to brush it off as if it didn't bother him. He actually went back to playing with KJ while Amanda dried herself from the shower.

Amanda took a deep breath because she almost ruined Keith trust *again* by secretly texting Steven! The family ate dinner that night and went to bed. To Amanda's surprise, Keith never brought up the issue concerning the texts.

12

BLACK ROSES

Three weeks had passed and Keith still had not said a word to Amanda about the text message incident with her ex Steven. Amanda recently accepted another position as a nurse in a small nursing home just outside of Raleigh, only twenty minutes from home. She was not only excited for the new position but also for a higher salary as a manager. Her new hours were 8:30 am to 5:00 pm. As for Keith, he began to take on more classes at Wake Tech and stayed productive until the opportunity to get back into law enforcement became available. KJ was growing up and was now walking. Since KJ was able to walk, he was able to attend a particular daycare center during the daytime hours.

One Friday night while sitting in the den, Amanda seemed very busy working on her laptop while Keith was in the kitchen with KJ. The father and son were watching one of KJ's favorite cartoons, SpongeBob Square Pants, on television. KJ began getting irritated because he was *fighting sleep*. He quickly jumped down from Keith's lap, ran into the den, and jumped in Amanda's lap. KJ started hugging his mother tightly briefly interrupting her workflow. Amanda found a place to save her work and began singing the alphabet song with KJ. After only five minutes, he fell fast asleep in her arms. Keith looked over and saw KJ sleeping in Amanda's arm. She was dozing off too. He walked into the den and quietly asked her to put him to bed since it was getting late. Keith told her since KJ was asleep, he wanted to do a quick workout before he going to bed. Amanda agreed and slowly lifted herself off the couch with KJ and made her way to KJ's bedroom.

Keith began a callisthenic work out in the den while watching the Los Angeles Lakers play against the San Antonio Spurs. He loved watching sports with the volume low and his music in his headphones on high! It was just his thing to do. It made him feel like he was in a gym. About thirty minutes into his workout, Keith paused his music and workout to get some water from the kitchen facet. He placed his headphones around his neck and reached for a glass from the cabinet above the facet. Keith was pouring in sweat while wearing his favorite grey tank top. He just needed a quick water-break before finishing his last set.

He filled the glass halfway with water. After drinking it all, he sat the glass on the table by the refrigerator.

While in the kitchen, Keith decided to go check on Amanda since she never came back into the den to finish her work on her laptop. As he walked down the hallway, he softly called for her, "Amanda…Amanda…yo Amanda?" There was no answer. He walked into KJ's room to check on him first but KJ was not in his room. He walked into their bedroom and there laid Amanda and KJ. They were sound asleep on the king-sized bed. Amanda was so tired; she didn't have the energy to put KJ into his bed. She had apparently already taken a shower and had on her pink pajamas while re-runs of SpongeBob played on the TV.

Keith started to wake her up but decided to wait until he finished working out. He began planning in his head that after he worked out he would put KJ in his bed. After putting him to bed, he would slowly take off Amanda's clothes to get his freak on! That would definitely wake her up! While standing at the door, he smiled briefly at the site of his lovely wife and son. A beautiful site that would touch the heart of any man. Reality was finally sinking in for Keith. He really was a family man now. He stood there for a while taking it all in then walked back towards the den to finish his workout. As he walked back down the hall, he placed his headphones back on his head. He just needed to finish his last set of push-ups before becoming the freak for his wife! He walked through the kitchen towards the den. It was the same path he took to get to the bedroom. He sipped some more water and began his last set of push-ups.

After five minutes, he was finished with his last set and his workout was now complete, Keith took off his headphones and turned the television s volume up to watch the last quarter of the basketball game. He figured he would watch the last few minutes while stretching his tight muscles.

While he watched to the game, Keith heard a low-pitched sound coming from Amanda's laptop. It was located on the other side of the den about fifteen feet away from him. It was a low sound but loud enough for Keith to recognize that the sound was the sound of an *instant message alert*. Keith stopped stretching and stood to his feet. He slowly walked over to Amanda's laptop and checked to see who the notification was from. By this time, it was after 10:00 p.m. He sat in the chair in front of the laptop and moved the mouse because the screen was black. Then he saw the screensaver of their family portrait.

When the laptop screen finally opened, Keith was able to see the notification alert. He clicked on icon. The notification was an email response from Steven! Amanda and her ex had stopped communicating through texting

SEDUCTION

and was now *secretly* emailing each other through her work email and personal! She had both emails browsers opened. Like sending *top-secret* information, they changed the mode of communication from verbal to email. However, this notification was from her personal email account. She had sent Steven a picture of herself standing in front of a mirror. Not only did she take a picture of herself in front of a mirror but she took the picture in front of the mirror in *their* bathroom, which was next to *their* bed! Stevens' email read:

> *"Damn Claire, you're still looking good...You don't even look like you had a baby. I bet I can still pick you up with one arm! I can't wait to see you again. Where are you at right now? Are you at work? I can stop by to see you like last time if you want? Funny how they really thought I was your brother-in-law! Lemme know something!*
> *–Yours Always "*

Keith read their entire conservation on both email accounts from his wife and her ex. He got so full of emotions! He became angry and hurt at the same time. He had so many thoughts going through his head. In the heat of passion, he thought of doing the worse to both of them (Amanda and her ex) and to get it all over with. Then he immediately thought of his son KJ! He couldn't let his son grow up without his father. Seeing his father locked up behind bars would hurt him more than anything.

Keith's mother and father taught him to pray to God about all problems, but this was the breaking point for him. As he read the explicit dialogue between Amanda and her ex, tears started flowing down his cheeks down to his chin and onto his drenched tank top. The tears flowed uncontrollably down his face until it was impossible to differentiate between the tears and sweat.

Keith clinched his fist tight and bit his bottom lip from anger at what his eyes had seen and read on the laptop. He quietly walked outside through the backdoor of the house, and sat in his car. Once inside, he yelled and cried at the top of his lungs while looking up at the star-filled sky through the crystal-clear glass of his T-top Camaro. Keith nearly went into an anxiety attack from crying so hard. This was one of the few nights that none of his neighbors was outside. Only the sound of his neighbor's dog echoed back at him. After crying to the point where he was too weak to cry anymore, he slowly got out of the car, walked up to the steps at the front door of his house and sat on the steps.

He was still having flashbacks of seeing his wife's picture being sent to another man. After telling himself repeatedly, to calm down, he was able to catch his breath and get a hold of himself. Keith then lifted himself and staggered a little but caught his balance on the rail on the steps. He slowly walked towards the back of the house and walked back inside the house.

Even though he had just finished working out, he walked into the kitchen and poured a double shot of Hennessey. While sipping on the brown liquor and wiping the running nose from crying, Keith started questioning himself why he didn't see this coming? "How long has this shit been going on?" "Is she fucking this dude now?" "What the fuck did I do to deserve this shit?" Keith thought to himself. He totally ignored all of the red flags and tried to do the right thing by marrying Amanda. He really loved her and little KJ with all of his heart. Keith began to regret the days he would pass up or refuse to sleep with other women who literally threw themselves at him. They didn't care that he was married, they wanted him anyway.

Keith was trying to do the right thing by being faithful for so long, but now ….the table had turned. If she wanted to play that kind of game with him, he was ready to play the same game too. Keith sipped the last bit of Hennessy from the glass and laid on the couch in the den where he cried himself to sleep.

The next morning, Keith woke up and walked into the master bedroom. As he walked through the door of their bedroom, Amanda was surprisingly awake. She was lying beside KJ who was still sound asleep. She was on her phone apparently texting or on social media as Keith walked through the door. He looked at her and nonchalantly looked straight-ahead in the direction of the bathroom. "Well good morning to you too sir! You stink…. I can smell you from here," said Amanda trying to make Keith smile. Keith didn't crack a smile. As he walked by, he briefly replied in a deep low tone, "yep…." He slowly closed the door trying not to snap and got into the shower.

While in the shower, Keith began to think logically. He thought to himself of how long he could go before he snapped on Amanda? How long could he go before he should let her know that he discovered her mistrust and her possible infidelity? He thought to himself "Maybe they were just joking around. Maybe they haven't slept with each other yet. Did she send the photo and wrote those explicit messages because he was too *busy* being *busy* as a husband? Was he neglecting his wife when she needed him? Was she beginning to feel lonely and that's why she fell into the seduction of her ex? Was the chapter of love really closed between her and Steven?"

Keith began to blame *himself.* Maybe he was too busy chasing goals and neglecting his wife? However, the more he attempted to think logically, the angrier he got! Then he thought about the laptop! He could send all of the photos and emails to his email if he should ever need them for *evidence* later. He knew he better save them because no one would ever believe that the nice church-going, gospel singing, respected wife would do anything like this.

He hurried out of the shower and pretended that he needed to get clean sweatpants from the laundry room. He walked passed Amanda, who was still on her phone and laying in the bed. She didn't even look up when he passed in front of her. Keith was wrapped in only a towel and still wet. "Gotta get some clean sweats!" he said quietly as he passed her. He rushed down the hallway and into the den where her laptop was located. He sat, opened it, and turned it on. After a brief moment to warmup, the laptop was ready to use. Shit! Amanda had a password that had the screen locked. Keith tried twice to enter a password but they were the wrong ones. Then he remembered an old password she used a long time ago. Keith kept looking down the hallway to see if Amanda was coming. He entered the password he remembered and silently prayed for it to work. The last attempt worked! He quickly forwarded all of the conversations between Amanda and her ex to his email then deleted the sent messages so that she wouldn't know about it.

That would be a secret that Keith would carry in his heart for months without telling anyone. He debated whether to expose her secrets through social media so that people would get to know the REAL Amanda. He decided to keep all of his frustrations bottled up inside him. He went along and played the role as a *happy husband* and exceptional father. Keith attended church as usual. He really could have won an Oscar Award for best actor. But keeping his emotions and hurt bottled up *inside* of him without at least getting therapy, would *only* be the beginning of his demise.

13

SECOND CHANCE

Months later, Keith after much contemplating, Keith decided to apply for the North Carolina Highway Patrol. He felt he had nothing to lose. His first attempt to work for NCHP was unsuccessful because of his credit score but that did not stop Keith. He was determined now, more than ever, to get back into law enforcement. Besides KJ, his main motivation was his father Mr. James' near death experience with the drunk driver. Keith didn't want anyone to have to experience the hardship and hurt that his family experienced during that time.

After filing his taxes that year, Keith decided to use his entire income tax refund to repair his credit score. He was determined to do whatever he had to do to get his application approved. Keith resubmitted his application to NCHP and it was accepted. Keith was overjoyed at knowing that his plan worked. He felt he now was on his way to becoming a better provider for KJ and his family. The hiring process for becoming a North Carolina State Trooper took almost six months to complete. To pass the time, Keith decided to apply with the North Carolina State University as a campus security officer. Keith had a very charismatic personality that people loved about him. He applied at the university and was hired on the spot. He started working during the summer of that year as a regular security officer but quickly climbed the ladder. He was promoted to campus police. Keith finally got a chance to wear a real badge and carry a gun for the first time.

Like working at the hospital, Keith was beginning to fit right in while working at the college. He was a fast learner so it took him no time to get to know his way around the campus.

Like the staff at the hospital, Keith was the talk around the campus. He was the youngest officer. He was handsome and the young female students absolutely loved him. Keith enjoyed the attention he got from the staff and female students. They flirted with him and he flirted back. The only difference was the fact that he was married now and had a son. While most of the females on campus who flirted with Keith didn't care

SEDUCTION

about his married life, he did. He knew that the city of Raleigh was one of those cities where everybody knew somebody that knows somebody that may know him. He wasn't trying to get caught up especially with the possibility of becoming a state trooper on the line! NC State offered substantial savings for employees to attend college. Keith took full advantage of the opportunity by attending classes as possible.

Keith was beginning to become a very busy man again. He would go to work at the campus night then go to class during the morning. Amanda and Keith *seemed* to have a system down to set them up for success despite Keith's silent emotional hurt from months ago.

One day after getting home from working all night and attending class that morning, Keith arrived home just as the mail carrier arrived with the mail. As he got out of his car, the mail carrier saw Keith and handed him the mail for his address. Keith was very tired and half-sleepy while looking through the mail. As he walked towards the front door of his home, he saw a brown envelope from the North Carolina Highway Patrol. It had been weeks since he turned in his application. Keith was so busy with work and school and didn't realize how much time had flown by.

When he saw the letter from them, he immediately sobered up and prayed a hopeful prayer that this is the official letter of acceptance that he had been looking for! Keith opened the front door and took of his shoes while silently chanting a prayer. He threw the rest of the mail onto the glass table in the living room, walked into the den, sat down and took a deep breath.

Right before he opened the letter, his mind began to think back to the time when he failed the academy twice with the local police department. He remembered the sacrifices he made with this attempt with NCHP. As he opened the letter from NCHP. It read:

> *"Dear Keith James,*
> *Congratulations! You have been accepted into the upcoming basic class for the North Carolina Highway Patrol. You are to report to..."*

That was all Keith needed to read before he let out a loud yell from excitement! Deep down inside, Keith was weighed down with the weight of two past failures at the academy and how he failed in nursing school. Keith was weighed down with silent pains of disappointment. However, he refused to quit and decided to give it one more chance and now... it paid off big time! Keith called his mom, dad, brother and last but not the least... Amanda. They all were very excited for him. Amanda was a bit busy with work and couldn't talk too long but when she heard the great news, she was more than excited for Keith!

Secretly, Amanda had been praying for Keith to get another chance at law enforcement. She remembered the look on his face after the two failed attempts. After she hung up the phone with Keith, she began crying at work over the good news! The acceptance was right on time for Keith. He felt so proud to do something his son KJ would be proud of!

After the mini celebration, Keith sat down on the couch. Keith was excited and nervous at the same time. He was excited to be accepted to become North Carolina's finest but also nervous at the same time about his home life. Keith would be away from his family for close to thirteen months! He would be able to come home on the weekends but to him, that would be a long time away from home. Especially since he had trust issues with Amanda.

Keith sat on the couch and briefly wondered if Amanda would stay committed to him knowing that he wouldn't be there to intercept her text or emails. He started to feel some anxiety about the time away from home. In the same breath, he now has a determination and obligation to KJ! Keith thought of how much it would mean for him to see KJ at his graduation! How cool it would be to take him to school in the patrol car and have other kids thinking KJ was the coolest kid because his dad was a state trooper. Keith thought about his father's near death experience with a drunk driver.

"If she's not gonna be trustworthy while I'm away at training, then I've got to do this for my son and I. It would be her loss… not mine!" Keith said to himself. He knew that things around the house was about to change… especially for him!

14

THE CALM BEFORE THE STORM

Keith entered training with the North Carolina Highway Patrol. He not only passed every exam, but also excelled as a leader while in training. It was a rough journey for Keith and Amanda while he was away at basic training. Amanda had to do her best with KJ at home while Keith was away at training. On the weekends, Keith would come home from training and get into so many arguments with Amanda over small things. Keith started the arguments mainly from his theory of possible mistrust from Amanda while he was away. It was pretty hard for the two of them, but after thirteen months of going through the toughest training the state of North Carolina had to offer, Keith made it. He graduated the North Carolina Highway Patrol basic training!

Keith was now a North Carolina State Trooper. It was a proud moment to see all of his family at graduation. Keith's parents, his brother, Amanda and little KJ. Even Keith's uncle and aunt came to see him graduate. It was such an exciting time. Keith was now embarking on a new journey as a state trooper.

Since his return from training, things were beginning to return to normal for Keith. KJ was now four years old. Keith was able to be home every day. But for some strange reason, to Keith, Amanda was becoming more secretive. She started becoming less and less intimate and affectionate towards Keith. They both had to get used to the other person being at home everyday verses just on the weekends.

One night, Keith attempted to be intimate with Amanda since KJ was spending the weekend at his grandparents' house. He stepped into the shower and knew Amanda needed to take one too. As she walked into the bathroom, Keith stepped out of the shower and dried off. Then he stood and leaned against the wall near the door. He let towel fall and just stood there butt-ass naked and watched Amanda undress. She looked over at Keith and smiled as if she was paying him no attention. Keith started moaning at each piece of clothing she removed until she was completely naked. She walked passed him. Keith reach to feel her ass but she slapped away his hand.

SEDUCTION

Amanda got into the shower and after about five minutes, she finally stepped out. Keith greeted her with a warm towel from the dryer. As he handed her the warm towel, Keith kissed her on her neck then her shoulder. Just when he attempted to make his next move to initiate intimacy, Amanda jumped away from Keith and laughed. "Stop playing now…" she said. But Keith wasn't playing, he was hornier than ever!

"Does it *look* like I'm playing with you?" said Keith while holding his erected dick. "My wife is *butt-ass naked* and my dick is harder than a fucking missile and you're gonna tell me to stop playing? Let me guess, you're *still* texting your ex, huh?" "What? No, I just don't feel like it tonight Keith! I'm going to bed… I'm tired!" Amanda replied while putting on the biggest underwear in her drawer.

Without even looking in Keith's direction, she put on sweat pants, a pink headscarf, and a white t-shirt then climbed into bed. Keith was still standing in the bathroom holding his manhood! Amanda's sex drive used to be pretty moderate but this was past ridiculous to Keith. She didn't even acknowledge him. It was as if he wasn't even there! Keith felt like he wasn't turning Amanda on anymore. He felt that maybe she wasn't attractive to him like she used to be. Amanda hadn't mentioned how much she loved him in months. She hadn't really shown him affection nor the attention that she used to show him when they were first married.

What Amanda didn't know was that Keith had a gut-feeling that she was possibly still texting her ex. Although Keith knew it wasn't healthy to be living in paranoia, his intuition that Amanda was still communicating with her ex was true. Keith was secretly observing Amanda's cell phone calls, text messages, and emails. He discovered more text messages from Amanda's ex in her cell phone. All of this had him wondering why were they were still fighting over this? They were married now but to Keith, nothing had really changed.

They argued so much about the whole ex situation until Keith decided to move out. He moved out and got an apartment about fifteen minutes from their home. He paid for the apartment for three months but only stayed a week in it. Keith's conscious about KJ possibly looking around the house kept bothering him. Because of how he was raised, Keith decided to go back home to be with his family, at least for KJ's sake.

However, things continued to spiral down. Keith and Amanda's communication was at its worse! Things remained the same. Things didn't go as Keith had hoped. He moved out again, this time he moved into a home with a co-worker and moved out for nearly three months. Even though he moved out, he made it his duty to see KJ daily. Little KJ was his heart! It didn't matter how busy Keith was

SEDUCTION

on the highway as a state trooper, he always made time to stop by KJ's daycare to see him. If Amanda wasn't busy, Keith would stop by the house to play with his little man.

With the threat of divorce on the brink, Keith's parents were now getting involved. His mom called him one night crying because of their situation. Keith was half-sleep in his room at his co-worker's home when she woke him with the call. She was crying because they saw the hurt and anguish Keith was going through, let alone little KJ. They really loved Amanda and knew that she was a good mother but they thought all of this was ridiculous. Then they started questioning Keith as if it was all his fault that he and Amanda were separated. His parents cried and constantly begged Keith to go back home. They wanted him to go back home and do the *right thing*. No matter how tough men are, no man ever wants to see or hear his mother cry.

So after hearing his mother cry over and over, Keith did just that. He went back home! He selfishly tried to deal with the fact that *communication* was not going well with he and Amanda. However, he didn't want to blame Amanda for it all. She was a decent woman and he was a good-guy but things were just falling apart over something Keith considered to be very *simple*. They decided to try marriage counseling. Amanda went to her pastor at her church and set an appointment for them. When Keith realized that the pastor was taking the side of Amanda, he got upset and quickly ended the session. He literally walked out! "Why should he waste his time listening to a man who was more concerned with who gave the most money to the church verses focusing on finding authentic answers for their problem?" thought Keith.

15

UNLEASH THE BEAST

One day Keith came to the unfortunate conclusion; if the text messaging between Amanda and her ex wasn't going to stop, maybe he should do his *own thing* too! Why should he allow his trust in Amanda to be mishandled and disrespected? People saw them and figured they were such beautiful/happy couple but Keith knew better. *Looks can truly be very deceiving.* At this point, Keith felt there was only so much disrespect he would take from Amanda and her ex.

※

Driven by this type of thinking, Keith became *bitter* towards Amanda. His heart began to grow cold with feelings of regret. This was not the same Amanda he had fell in love with years ago. "People change, but one's respect for another shouldn't, especially in a marriage. Shit, I should've paid attention to all those damn *warning* signs! Oh well, fuck it!" Keith said to himself. It was then that it became official, the BEAST that was lying dormant for years, was about to be unleashed. Keith resurrected his former lifestyle of being a player.

Keith decided to start a social media page. He had a profile page set up in no time! Keith profile consisted of only photos of him and KJ. He even had a relationship status of being "single". Keith was now a *scarred man* who wanted the feeling of *worth* from someone. This was an old but new territory for him. He had suppressed his *player's-card* before marriage but now he had released the kraken!

While online, Keith was able to meet women from all over the United States and even across the Atlantic. From a heart filled with signs of mistrust, Keith began privately messaging females locally and aboard. If he didn't privately message them, they secretly instant messaged him. Keith began to dress better and groomed himself daily. Amanda was used to seeing Keith groomed and dressed so it wasn't anything new to her. Keith became *less argumentative* towards her. He no longer looked through her cell phone.

Now that this silent-hurting man was on the loose, Keith started to *see* other females. Not just any females. Keith was exclusively seeing: nursing students, nurses, college girls, sorority girls, white women, black women, Latino women, professional women and models. All of which knew he was married but never said a word about their secret affair with him. If Keith didn't care, why should they? Keith kept in mind all the times he came home and Amanda brushed him off as though he didn't exist. Only this time, Keith wasn't *begging* for her attention anymore. Keith had found other women who would pay *attention* to him. Keith never had a hard time finding a date or someone to flirt with but since home wasn't being taking care of, he search for what he wanted outside of it. Keith's *mentality* now was that if he wanted it, he would get it even if he had to get it from someone else.

Keith would leave home to make trips to Walmart at night only to have a *quickie* or make phone calls to other females. Some nights Keith would make sure KJ and Amanda were sound asleep then sneak away for thirty minutes or so just to have a sexual encounter. He had women who would unapologetically let him sneak over in the middle of the night or meet him at his beckon call. They didn't care where the settings was, they just *liked being* with Keith. In his car, against his car's hood, on a dark backroad, behind closed doctor's offices, in their homes while their boyfriends were at work… it didn't matter. Keith got it *whenever* he wanted it.

If he only wanted his cock sucked, they would do it without complaining or having him *beg* for it. If he just wanted a quickie, all he had to do was say the word and they would be waiting for him with no underwear. Keith would have nights where he dressed in his patrol uniform, as though he was "called into work" at the last minute, only to stay with another *female* for the night. Then he would return the next morning around his normal time, in uniform as though nothing happened.

The funny thing was; Keith never made love to these women, he just *fucked* them. He simply found *relief* from his silent frustrations of his home life by giving them rough sex or letting them please him. They all knew he was married and could *sense* that he was also unhappily married. They complied willingly to *make* him happy. Keith was becoming a beast with all these sexual escapades.

One day while alone at home, Keith saw Amanda's personal email account was open on the desktop computer in the den. He hadn't checked her email in a while since the old Keith was resurrected. Although he was living a secret live, he still loved Amanda and wanted to see if things had slowed down between her and her ex. He had made up his mind that if he didn't see any messages between them, then he would slowdown or consider stopping some of those secret escapades. As he logged in, he immediately noticed a new file located under her inbox. Keith clicked on the file and saw a picture of a guy's cock. He researched the sender's name and searched him on Facebook. It was a guy he remembered from a local cell phone store. "What the FUCK?" Thought Keith.

Things were getting so out of control on BOTH ends. Keith was working *protecting* and *serving* the community, but not even protecting and serving his own house. Amanda was portraying to be a good, church-going, innocent wife but was also living a double life. Their marriage seemed not to matter to either of them anymore.

To get his mind off things at home, Keith decided to re-enlist into the United States Air National Guard near Raleigh, SC.

While at drill, he cheated as many times as he possibly could. Military women who understood his home-situation because they had similar situations of their own. And if they didn't care, neither did Keith. A hurting man *plus* a hurting wife and the lack of *trust* and *communication*, made their home a living hell.

Keith's main concern through all of this was not Amanda, but his son KJ. All he desired at this point was to be a better father to him. Keith desired to be in KJ's life just as his dad was for him while growing up. Keith really loved Amanda but because of the uncertainty their trust, he was having the feeling that he didn't want to be with her anymore. When they all were home, they walked around the house like prisoners in a jail cell. With the exception of KJ, one said, "I love you" or hugged anymore.

Most nights, Keith would sleep on the couch or cuddled with KJ in his twin bed. While in public, they played the part of *being* happily married. They could have easily won the Oscar Award for "Couple of the Year". However, at home they were secretly *suffering*. While at work, Keith would lock drunk drivers up for crimes only to face the fact that the people who wore the handcuffs were only a *reflection* of his emotional self. Amanda was busy taking care of patients who needed medical care only to realize that her *home* was not being taken care of either. They both were eating, sleeping, and breathing *silent frustration*.

One evening, Keith tried to be intimate with Amanda while KJ was away at his grandparents' home. It had been a while since the two were intimate. That night, he tried kissing Amanda and different places of her body but it all felt foreign to both of them. It just didn't feel right to *either* one of them. Amanda couldn't even look Keith in the eyes while in the missionary position. They both knew that *it* wasn't there anymore. What was once a *spark* was now just a sad and *extinguished flame.* The glorious glow that they once had in their eyes for one another was now a distant memory. While in intercourse, Amanda moaned and gave a slight exhalation from a mini orgasm that felt forced.

Keith climaxed but it was short-lived with no energy or force behind it. They had the most lackluster sex imaginable. The sex felt less than animalistic. Lifeless.

After the brief and lifeless session, they both turned away from each other and slept with their backs turned to one another. No one needed to turn the lights off in the room because their souls were already dark with *mistrust, hurt,* and *miscommunication.*

16

BLURRED LINES

Well, a few weeks later, Amanda called Keith around midday and told him she had a surprise for him! Keith was home enjoying a day off from work. He went outside and began washing his patrol car. Amanda called about an hour later and said she was getting off work soon and that she said she would pick up KJ from the daycare. Keith went inside and took a shower to wash away the dirt that accumulated from washing his car. By the time Keith finished showering, Amanda and KJ had arrived home and were entering the house through the front door.

Keith was putting on a tank top and sweat pants when they came into the bedroom. KJ ran and gave his father a hug then grabbed Keith's cell phone so he could play a video game. Amanda walked toward Keith with a smile on her face and a white plastic bag in her hand.

She reached over and handed it to him. Keith sat on the edge of the bed holding what must have been the surprise she was referring to earlier. He anticipated that she went to her favorite underwear store and bought something to spice up their bedroom like some laced panties or lingerie. While he held the bag with a confused look on his face, Amanda reached into the white plastic bag and pulled out a sheet of paper that read, "Congratulations DADDY!"

Keith looked at Amanda with disbelief and said, "What is this?" Amanda replied, "Keith, what does it look like? Duh…. I'm pregnant!" With a look of confusion and disappointment, Keith said, "What? What do you mean you're pregnant? I don't even remember *cum'n* the last time we had sex!" "Well, that's what happens when two people have sex!" Amanda sarcastically replied as she prepared to take a shower.

While playing the game on Keith's cell phone, KJ asked, "Daddy, what's coming?" Keith briefly laughed at KJ's statement then snuffed KJ across his head and said, "I'm coming to get my cell phone, so you better hurry up and play that game before I do!" Meanwhile, Keith has all kinds of thoughts going through his head. Nothing criminal, just thoughts about paternity that no man should have to think about when his *wife* says that she's pregnant.

Keith started thinking about all the messages and pictures he discovered on Amanda's laptop. Keith couldn't help but ponder two simple questions in his head. What if this baby isn't his? What if she was sleeping around with her ex and was trying to cover it up by claiming him as the father? Keith had the evidence of her *possible* infidelity from her text messages and emails forwarded to his email. He even had the conversations with her and the guy from the cell phone store. He had all kind of evidence that suggested she was sleeping around. Evidence that *suggested* a possibility that this baby may *not* belong to him.

༄

While he pondered over these thoughts, he realized that he couldn't put *all* the blame on Amanda. She had also gone through so much in the marriage. He took her though so many transitions while they were together. Leaving her for long periods of time to take care of the home and KJ while away in training. He had let her down so many times. They *both* were doing wrong things! He knew he had messed up and she had messed up too secretly *too*. In his mind, she messed up, he messed...they were even. He wasn't about to put all the blame on her for her actions. However, when there is a baby in the picture, it changes the rules.

SEDUCTION

While the thought of having a new baby should have been wonderful news to the young married couple, Keith and Amanda were anything but happy. Amanda seemed pretty happy but Keith wasn't happy at all about the news. Keith was still in shock that Amanda was pregnant! "With all the lack of trust and loyalty between the two, how could he be so confident at this moment?' He thought.

Soon the word got out about Amanda being pregnant. Everywhere he and Amanda went, people would congratulate them on their new addition to the family. The ones congratulating them were mostly Amanda's friends. Keith didn't tell a *soul* about the pregnancy. He wanted to share the news with everyone he knew. He wanted the feeling of passing out cigars and celebrating the moment with loved-ones, his friends and coworkers. He wanted to share the news with at least his family. Keith thought of how happy his parents would be if they knew that they had a new grandchild on the way. But he said nothing.

When Amanda's friends congratulated Keith, he would smile and say *'thank you'* passively. Keith was beginning to show signs of uncertainty while being alone with Amanda. She could feel his coldness when sleeping next to her. During the night, Keith would toss and turn from worrying and frustration. When he couldn't sleep, he would get up, walk in the den and watch ESPN or a movie.

Every night that he got out of bed or toss and turned, Amanda knew it. She pretended most nights to be asleep but was awake silently wishing Keith would stay in bed with her. She just wanted him to comfort her by wrapping his arms around her as she slept next to him. She knew deep down that Keith had unfortunately lost trust in her. She knew that he had seen the emails exchanged between her and her ex Steven. She knew that he had seen the photos and read the texts of their secret visitations. Instead of confronting Keith about not sleeping with her, she would just lay squeezing her pillow tight under her face. Her pillow stayed soaked most nights from tears of loneliness.

She needed to feel the touch and caress from her man. The touch that a pregnant woman needed from her man and it pegged her that she was alone. Her hormones were out of control and the only comfort she now felt was from a pillow, which could not talk back. As she squeezed the pillow, she thought back at the one incident at the traffic light when her and her ex-boyfriend made eye contact. She really thought that the chapter of love and emotions from their five-year history between them was closed.

She was known in the church to be a very decent woman. She was a part of the praise dancers, and a person of good-standing within the community. Now, she found herself bracing the possibility of being a divorced mother with two children simply because she ruined the trust of her husband.

Every night when Keith would get out of bed in the middle of the night, Amanda would also awake and they would both be on two different ends of the house crying themselves to sleep.

17

THE OSCAR AWARD COUPLE

Four months later, Amanda was beginning to show signs of being pregnant. Now everyone pretty much knew that they were expecting a new addition to their young family. Periodically, Amanda would ask Keith to bring her lunch at her job. As soon as Keith walked up to her office, all of Amanda's co-workers, which were mostly women, would hug and congratulate Keith. When they went to church, the pastor and church members would congratulate them. While in the grocery store, they would run into some of Amanda's friends who would ask if they had chosen a name for their child. They wanted to know if there were dates for the baby-shower or baby's registry information.

During those moments, as difficult as it was, Keith would just play the part of the *happy* husband and father-to-be. He could have easily received an Oscar Award for his stellar performance. But it was during those times that Keith started having emotional breakdowns *away* from home. He felt so embarrassed. He didn't know how long he could keep those feelings bottled up inside of his heart.

"Shit, what am I going to do if this baby isn't *mine*? How the hell am I going to explain this to my family and friends? Should I even stay married?" Were just a few of the many racing thoughts running laps in Keith's head. Mistrust, lack of communication, and now this paternity issue were not only negatively affecting Keith's mental health but also his safety. He began losing concentration while working the dangerous highways as a state trooper. At night, he would find a quiet place to park his patrol car just so he wouldn't have to talk to people or let people see him.

However, Keith never let his emotions affect his uniform appearance. He remained sharp in appearance as usual but his work performance fell *drastically*. He was depressed most days and emotionally unfit for patrolling the dangerous highways. However, Keith was very good at masking his emotions. To the outside world, he was okay but he was far from being okay! Other than his work performance, Keith was still a "pretty boy" on the police force, but he was just hiding behind his contagious smile.

One night Keith's patrol supervisor met with him to discuss his job performance. He was Caucasian male in his mid-forties and was recently been promoted to the supervisor position. He always respected Keith and always warned him if things were not going well around the office. "Keith, I'm concerned about you brother. You haven't been yourself lately. Everyone in positions above me are giving me hard time about your job performance. They are becoming very concerned about you too. If there is anything I can do to help you brother, just let me know." With yet another award-winning performance, Keith assured him that the poor job performance was just from the re-adjustment of Amanda being pregnant and that he was *fine.*

Desperately attempting to *increase* his job performance, Keith began to stop as many cars as he could stop during his shift just to make it *look* like he was staying busy during the night. Even though his job didn't have a quota, Keith knew that if he could stop at least ten cars in a shift, that would be enough to keep them off his back. He figured if he could do it within the first three to four hours of work, then he could find a quiet place to gather his thoughts for the rest of the night.

The next night at work, Keith stopped eleven cars within the first three hours. He had achieved his desired number and was now hiding in his normal hide out spot. He was depressed and he knew it. Most nights he mainly wished the shift would hurry up and end so he could go home and sleep on the couch while Amanda was away at work. His mind was constantly racing with negative thoughts about his home. He tried meditation but that didn't work. Keith tried to put on some hardcore rap music while driving at night but that didn't work either. Even while listening to the rap music, his mind would go back to the uncertainty of his child.

While raining one night, Keith was dispatched to a wreck about ten miles from his hideout spot. "Dammit!" yelled Keith after receiving the call. He sped out of his hideout spot like Batman from his cave and responded to the wreck scene. When he arrived on the scene of the wreck, he immediately saw what appeared to be the driver of the wrecked car standing near the scene talking with deputies. The driver looked drunk because he was staggering and could barely keep his balance.

Two local county deputies had detained the drunk driver until Keith arrived as the investigating trooper. "Look at this shit… how the hell do you wreck on this lonely ass country road?" said Keith as he prepared to get out of his car. As soon as Keith stepped out of his patrol car, the drunk driver looked over and started heckling Keith. Keith calmly asked the deputies to remove the handcuffs from the drunk driver so he could offer him a sobriety test.

As soon as they took the handcuffs off him, the drunk driver rushed towards Keith to attack him. Keith anticipated the rush and took one step to the side and caught the drunk driver in mid-strive. Keith picked the driver up in the air and body slammed him on the side of the highway! The drunk driver then lifted his head out of the muddy surface and started apologizing immediately to Keith. Trooper Keith James was not in good mood and the deputies saw it. Keith was so full of anger and frustration prior to his arrival to the scene and this drunk driver was his outlet for the night. He put his handcuffs on the drunk driver, placed him in his patrol car and closed the door.

"Got damn Keith, you picked his ass up and slammed him... and your ass is STILL CLEAN? You ain't playing no games tonight I see!" said one of the deputies. Keith just shook his head and wiped the small amount of mud off his shoes. He finished the report then took the driver to jail.

18

THE MISTRESS

About thirty minutes later, Keith had booked the drunk driver at the jail and was heading back to his favorite hideout spot. He had stopped eleven cars and booked a drunk driver! His night was 100% done! He wasn't about to stop another car for the rest of the night. While Keith was on his way to his *spot*, he received another call from dispatch advising him of another wreck. "Fuuuuuuck my life!" yelled Keith in disappointment!

The call was for a driver who had hit a deer thirty miles west from the city of Raleigh. Keith had recently left the jail in Raleigh and was not even remotely close to that area. Just as he picked up the microphone to radio back to the dispatcher, another trooper, who was closer, took the call. This meant Keith didn't have to go to the scene. "Hell yeah!" he said while cruising towards his hideout spot.

While on the way, Keith listened to the description of the call as it was given to the other trooper. The dispatcher said that someone had hit a deer but no one was hurt in the accident. The dispatcher then gave the name over the radio and the driver's contact number. The dispatcher told the trooper that the person's name was "Whitney Carter and her number is area code (310)232-..."

Side Note

Rewind the time to about two months prior to this night. Keith really started hanging out more on social media. He befriended so many people on there. He had seen a profile of a beautiful girl named Whitney Carter on there and befriended her. She was very pretty and a model for a fitness magazine. Keith admired her confidence. She accepted and they became online friends. She somewhat reminded him of the singer Beyoncé Knowles. Keith started researching where she was from. She was from Los Angeles, CA. Apparently, she had family staying in the Raleigh area so every now and again she would fly over to visit. A few weeks after befriending her online, as fate would have it, Keith was off duty getting gas at a local gas station. While paying for gas, guess who walked in? Ms. Whitney Carter.

Keith didn't want to sound stalk-ish, so he decided to nonchalantly speak to her. He deepened his voice and said, "Hey, you're Whitney right?" She replied with a smile, "Hi, yeah....how did you know?" "Hi, I'm Keith; I'm your friend on Instagram." She smiled and said, "Oh... okay, nice to meet you." She seemed to be in a rush to pay for gas. He reached out and shook her hand. They exchanged smiles and she left. She had on regular clothes but damn she was so fine! As she left, Keith had a feeling that he would definitely see her again.

*Now back to *this* night (two months after meeting her at the gas station)*

When Keith heard her name called over the radio, he was surprised! It was Whitney and she was back in Raleigh! This time she was in trouble. She must have hit a deer while driving home to her parents' home. Keith remembered that they were friends on social media. He figured she probably wasn't logged on but decided to contact her anyway. So Keith, messaged her in her DM.

"Hey Whitney, this is Keith. I'm the guy who you met at the gas station across the street from the mall in Raleigh a few months ago. The guy who probably came off as being stalk-ish. lol Anyway, I am a state trooper. I'm working tonight and just heard your name on the radio. Looks like you hit a deer. Are you okay?"

To Keith's surprise, she immediately responded.

"Hey! Yeah, that was me who hit the deer. I'm okay though, thank you for reaching out! I really hate that I hit that deer! I cried all the way home. Anyway, I didn't know you were a state trooper! That's pretty cool!"

Keith could tell by reading her messages that she was still very emotional from hitting the deer and that she was a lover of animals. After a while, he was able to calm her down by direct messaging her. Before they knew it, he and Whitney were flirting. They exchanged telephone numbers and it was on from there.

꧁

Keith knew he was very *vulnerable* emotionally from Amanda being pregnant and the paternity issue, but he felt a slight sigh of *relief* to meet someone. However, in Keith's mind, Whitney would be just another "jumpoff". Someone he would sleep with for a few months then let go.

He only wanted *temporary relief* from the issues he had at home with Amanda. However, the more he and Whitney exchanged text or talked on the phone, the more they became attracted to each other. Whitney told Keith that she had just moved back to Raleigh to stay with her parents. She was taking some time off before her next photo shoot for a magazine. She told him that she would be staying with them for a few months. This was great news to Keith. He was hoping to get to know her for a few months anyway. Whitney was a breath of fresh air to Keith. He had a reason to smile again. As weeks went by, Keith and Whitney began flirting intensely. He really wanted Whitney physically, but refused to show any signs of desperation. Keith knew how to play hard to get. It was his way of getting his way with females. He knew if he kept playing hard to get with Whitney, he would be intimate with her in no time.

19

WAIST DEEP

As weeks past, Keith started grooming himself again. He began working out more. He started keeping his car clean like he used to do when he first met Amanda. This was beginning to feel like deja'vu to Keith. He was doing the exact same thing after meeting Amanda. Keith was a Capricorn, looking good was important to him. Having a close-to-perfect image was mandatory for him. Since the time Keith and Whitney met, their conversations became *very* steamy! The conversations were getting so steamy to the point Keith started to keep the ringer of his cell phone on vibrate or silence when he was around Amanda and while sleeping at night.

Whitney was a model for a fitness magazine. She loved sending Keith pictures of herself wearing gym gear but always posed in the most seductive way. Their initial correspondence were honest and innocent text messages. Then it led to smiley faces, which led to pictures. Then they began *sexting*. Whitney began sending Keith whatever type of picture he wanted from her. If he wanted a picture of her working out, she would send him a picture. If he wanted one of her playing with *herself*, she would send it. If he wanted only a picture of *her*, she would send it. A full body shot of her standing in front of the mirror completely naked was her favorite picture to send to him. Hell, she was a model and she knew what she was working with.

Keith started thinking about testing the waters. Should he send a picture of *himself* to her? He was starting to feel that it would only be fair since she was sending so many pictures of herself to him.

After a few more seductive pictures from Whitney, he finally built up the courage to send her a picture of...*him*. Keith wasn't nervous about sending a picture of himself because he had a *small man*... nah, that wasn't even the case. Keith was well endowed. He was a bit nervous because he had never sent a picture of that area of his body to no one else but his wife. *But* if Amanda was sending naked pictures to her ex Steven while she was still married to Keith and getting pictures of another guy's cock in her email, Keith figured what did he have to lose?

Keith waited until Amanda left for work one morning and decided to finally take the picture of *himself.* He went in the guest bathroom, lowered his sweat pants, and pulled it out. Keith always shaved down there and never wore underwear so it was easy access for him to get to it. He picked up his phone and found Whitney's name in his contact list. He took the picture...and then hit *send*. After sending the picture, Keith took a deep breath and let out a sigh of relief that he finally did it.

Although Keith was hesitant to send Whitney the picture, to him it felt like total *revenge* against Amanda. He felt like it was her karma for her secret life. There she was sending photos of herself to her ex while he was out risking his life on the dangerous highways, why should he feel *bad* about sending it? If this was the kind of game she wanted to play, then so be it! After thinking about what Amanda did behind his back, Keith felt no remorse.

After about five minutes of no response from Whitney, Keith started getting a bit nervous. As second thoughts about sending the picture started to creep in, she finally replied. She replied just the way Keith knew she would respond. She responded with about twelve emoji of a tongue hanging out to suggest that she really liked what she saw! After *seeing* what they both were working with, Keith and Whitney talked about planning a day to finally meet each other in person. Whitney sent Keith her parents address.

Three days later Keith made plans to meet up with Whitney. He figured that meeting her in the evening while working would be the best time. He couldn't think of a better time to meet her for the first time than while working. Quite frankly, meeting her while working was his only option. As a trooper, he traveled hundreds of miles per shift, so stopping by to see Whitney would not be a problem.

When the opportunity arrived for Keith to see her, he sped down the highway to get to her before his next call came across the radio. It was after 10 pm before he could get over to see Whitney. It was pretty cold outside that night. The temperature was around 35 degrees. That is *pretty cold* for the south! He called her while he was on the way. During their brief conversation, they both agreed that they would hold their first conversation in his car since it was getting late. This would also be the most private way since she was staying with her parents. Plus, they didn't want to have any interruption if one grabbed the other and started feeling on the other.

Keith finally arrived at Whitney's address. He was a bit nervous but confident to meet her. He and Whitney had exchanged so many text messages between them over the past few weeks. All that was left to do was for them to meet face to face! When he arrived in the driveway, he texted her:

"Hey, I'm here… my apologies for being so late… it's been a busy night."
"It's okay, I'm coming out now!" she replied.

Keith waited in his warm patrol car for about three minutes in anticipation of Whitney's arrival. While waiting, he silently prayed that he wouldn't get a call from his dispatcher…or Amanda. If he got either one of those, it would mess up his chance to spend time with Whitney. He and Whitney had been texting and sexting intensely for the last two weeks now and they both were anticipating seeing each other!

Finally, Whitney opened the door and walked out of the house. Keith wanted to get out of his car and give her a hug but remained in the car playing it cool. Since it was pretty cold that night, he had the inside of his car nice and warm. As she got closer to the patrol car to get in, Keith looked on in amazement. She was a bit taller than he had expected. She looked 5ft 6' in her pictures but in person she was close to 5f 9'. Everything looked better in person. He leaned over and opened the passenger's door to let her in.

Whitney sat down gracefully in the front passenger seat and closed the door. They immediately looked at each other and started smiling. This was their first time really *seeing* each other. The first time was very brief at the gas station but now they both were really seeing each other. They looked at each other again and started shaking their head simultaneously. They weren't shaking their head in disappointment, they both were both relieved that the other *actually* looked like the photos they had on social media.

Keith reached across the equipment in the center and gave Whitney a hug. Whitney started the conversation. While Whitney was talking, Keith was already thinking about being intimate with her. Whitney was wearing a tight mini t-shirt with no bra and tight pink yoga pants. It was cold outside and her nipples puckered through her t-shirt. Keith nodded at Whitney while she was talking but silently wished she would shut up so he could kiss her. Whitney, feeling Keith's strong sexual energy spiking, stopped talking and gazed at Keith. Then she briefly looked around his car. She had never been in a state trooper's car before. She never had a reason to. Keith began conversing but was interrupted by his dispatcher. A wreck had occurred on the other side of Raleigh towards Durham. But before Keith could respond to the call, another trooper responded that he was closer and would handle it. So far, luck was on their side!

Keith didn't have to leave. Hearing Keith's deep voice over the radio, plus seeing the guns and blue lights all around was turning Whitney on! She was getting so horny at the thought of seeing Keith in his element...and in his uniform. She could literally see his dick-print in his pants while he was sitting behind the steering wheel. Keith stopped talking as he felt her vibes toward him. He looked over at Whitney and saw her eyes dilated with strong sexual energy towards him. She was biting her bottom lip and rubbing both thighs with her hands.

Keith changed the subject by asking Whitney about her day. He was the king of distraction and he knew it. If a girl was getting aroused by him, he knew how to distract her just to heighten her arousal. After a low-pitched sigh, she reluctantly began explaining her day. But by the time Whitney got to her second sentence, Keith reached over and grabbed her gently by her neck and slowly kissed her. Whitney was literally *taken* by surprise. She began to moan at Keith's boldness how he just took the opportunity to kiss her. She was hoping that he would have kissed her earlier but his timing could not have been better.

While kissing, they both began to flashback to the text messages and pictures. Their kissing began to get very heated. Keith was now caressing her breast. He started kissing her bottom lip and then her chin. He kissed his way down her neck and passed her clavicles. Keith then reached and pulled Whitney's hair back and exposed her left breast. He slowly began licking her nipple. He started twirling his tongue in circles in a way that seemed to hypnotize her. Whitney reached into her yoga pants felt her heated feminine liquid slowly flowing. Then said, "Oh my god, I'm so wet right now! You know you can't finish what you are starting! You ain't even right for this!"

࿔

Keith was a master at foreplay. His deep voice, tongue and hands were so talented. However, he knew that she wanted to return the favor to him. He leaned back in his patrol car and unzipped his pants. Keith wasn't playing! He slowly pulled out his cock. "Well damn, isn't he brave?" Whitney said to herself. Whitney rushed over to stroke his endowed cock. She was stroking a state trooper's cock while he was in full uniform and in a patrol car! Her head was spinning at the thought of it all. After a few long strokes from her, he could tell that she wanted to go down on him. Keith slowly grabbed her hand, moved it back onto her side of the car and put his cock back inside his pants. He smiled at her and said, "Not yet". "You're kidding right? You play too much Keith!" With a sad face, Whitney reluctantly agreed. The two were interrupted again by dispatch but this time Keith had to leave to respond to the call. The two kissed each other goodnight and parted ways. Their first official meeting was nothing short of what they both had anticipated it would be.

While Keith was on his way to the call, he reached for his for his cell phone and saw that he had four missed calls and six text messages from Amanda. She had called and text him while he was making out with Whitney. She had never called that many times in a row, especially at that time of night. It was as if she had a sixth sense that he was with someone else or had a private investigator tracking him. Keith called her back just to make sure KJ was okay. She answered,

"Umm, I've been trying to reach you, where you been?"

It was strange for Amanda to question him as he was while working. Maybe she did she have someone watching him! Not sure if she did or not, Keith calmly replied,

"I locked up a drunk driver and was at the jail. Everything okay?" Keith replied.

She said, "Yeah, just wanted to let you know that the baby was moving all around. It has been kicking me all evening and I couldn't sleep, but I'm getting sleepy now. Please be safe out there. See you in the morning. I'll try to have breakfast made for you. I love you."

"Okay, glad everything is *okay*... I love you too... see you in the morning then!"

"Goodnight", said Amanda.

"Goodnight" he replied.

SEDUCTION

Damn, that was close thought Keith. As soon as he hung up with Amanda, Whitney texted him. She wanted him to come back! Keith already know what she wanted if he came back. He texted her back and told her that he could not come back because the wreck would take a long time to complete. He just asked her to text him for the rest of the night until she fell asleep. She sent him a naked picture of herself sitting in front of a mirror holding her titty in one hand with a sad face.

Keith had to gather his thoughts together. He was battling so many thoughts. His mind was racing again. He was getting waist deep into another situation. He and Whitney were hitting it off so fast but he was still married to Amanda. How should he tell Whitney that he was married? How could he explain being unhappily married and having an uncertain paternity confirmation with his pregnant wife? Keith was a father who loved his son KJ. He was viewed within the community as a good man, a standup guy, and a family man. On top of that, his wife Amanda is pregnant and there is the paternity issue that was silently ached his heart.

※

"What is a man to do in situation like this?" He thought. "How should I handle all of this? It's too late to divorce Amanda for infidelity. Even if I divorced her, I would still be hated because most people believe that it's *always* the man's fault for a divorce." His thoughts were racing faster than ever now. The feelings he was starting to have towards Whitney, were the exact same feelings that he was missing with Amanda. Then there's KJ. The last thing Keith wanted was to have KJ grow up without his biological father in his life. He didn't want KJ to grow up and be a possible statistic as a fatherless child. If he stayed with Amanda and the baby she's pregnant with is not his, should he just deal with the issue silently?

Should he just stay around and live the rest of his life with an unhealthy secret? Their marriage would never be the same. Keith dealt with those thoughts while working on the dangerous highways as a state trooper. He was stopping cars during the day and late night hours while in silent frustration. He was so unfocused while dealing with criminals, which jeopardized his safety. There were several nights when Keith arrived home and couldn't even remember what transpired the night he worked. He was working dazed and vexed in his soul with so many secrets. Secrets he couldn't tell anyone, not even his parents or younger brother. He knew he had to do something before things get out of hand.

20

THE TRUTH HURTS

Weeks passed and the stinging reality of Amanda having the baby was getting closer and closer for Keith. Her due date was just around the corner. Amanda was now six months pregnant and was beginning to show signs more now than ever. Keith and Amanda were getting more congratulatory remarks now since they received the news that they were expecting a baby boy! They got more good news, this time Amanda would be able to go the full term with the pregnancy.

Family members were trying to help with picking a name for the new baby boy. Everyone was so happy for the young married couple. Guys within the community and other troopers would pat Keith on the back to show their support and happiness towards him. All of this attention was making Keith more stressed than ever. He started playing golf and working out more on his days off and while KJ was in school. He would do anything that would help keep his mind off the problem at home.

One Wednesday morning while playing golf, Whitney texted Keith to see what he was up to. He told her that he was out playing golf. Knowing that Keith was playing golf, she sent him a photo of her playing with *herself* in the mirror. Before the text, Keith was at even par through six holes on the front nine holes. When he opened the picture text and saw Whitney butt-ass-naked, he completely lost his focus! He sliced his next attempt at hitting the golf ball. They guys looked at Keith with a confused look. "What the hell was that Keith?" asked one of the guys. He shook his head then continued to play and finished the game.

It was then that Keith contemplated that if Whitney could distract him from his golf game, maybe he would use her as a *temporary distraction* from his problems at home. Keith texted her and said he wanted to take her on a date. Whitney didn't even hesitate; she agreed to go out with him. The following weekend, Keith told Amanda that he wanted to go out with his fraternity brothers Friday night to watch the game. He hadn't been out in a while. Amanda knew that going out with his frat brothers was something Keith needed. So she agreed that he should go chill with his brothers. When Friday came, instead of

SEDUCTION

hanging out with his frat brothers, Keith went and picked up *Whitney*. He had washed his car earlier that day so it was nice and clean for a night out on the town. When he arrived to her home, she got in his car gracefully looking like the model that she was.

Keith decided to take her to a seafood restaurant outside of Raleigh that was known for great food and low lighting. He didn't want to be anyway near Raleigh. Plus, he didn't want to run into anyone who may recognize him as Amanda's husband. Keith wanted to have good time with Whitney and figured this would be his chance to tell her about his "situation" at home. Keith and Whitney had intimate conversations while on the way to the restaurant. Whitney held Keith's hand and gazed at him the entire trip. She seem to be genuinely interested in Keith. She was beginning to have strong feelings toward Keith. Whitney was hurt from a previous relationship with a lawyer and was glad to find good, honest, and intimate conversations with a good man like Keith.

They finally arrived at the restaurant. The waiter escorted them to their seat. It felt like every man and woman focused their eyes on Whitney as she walked through the crowd following the waiter. She was wearing heels so she was tall, fit and angelic. The women's eyes were more fixated on her than the guys. Once seated, the two began to really hit it off! Considering this was only their first date, Keith and Whitney were hitting it off as though they had known each other for years. Neither of them were shy, reserved, or even hesitant around each other. They talked about everything that transpired from the night of Whitney's deer wreck to the first encounter at the gas station. They even talked about the distraction at the golf course and their first kiss in Keith's patrol car. The two laughed, kissed, gazed into each other's eyes, and held hands the entire time. Other couples in the restaurant observed their chemistry.

While sitting at the table, Whitney began talking about her future plans. While she was talking to Keith, his mind went back home to Amanda and KJ. He started thinking about how he and Amanda use to enjoy special nights like this. He started thinking about KJ being at home probably wondering where he was that night. Then Keith started thinking about Amanda, her being pregnant and the paternity issue. Keith who seemed dazed and in a hypnotic state of mind, knew it was time for him to be transparent with Whitney about his marriage.

He reached over and placed his right hand on top of Whitney's left hand while she was still talking to him. When he grabbed her hand and looked into her eyes, Whitney knew that there was something wrong with Keith. His countenance had drastically changed. As much as Keith tried to think of the best way to explain his situation

SEDUCTION

to Whitney. He didn't know how to start the conversation. Starting to visibly worry, she asked Keith if something was wrong. They had such a great conversation all evening until now. Keith had gotten serious so quick. Whitney began to think the worst!

Keith regained his composure, as he looked Whitney straight into her eyes. Then he asked, "Do you really want to be with me? If you do…how patient are you?" With a slightly confused look on her face, she replied, "What do you mean how patient am I Keith? What's wrong? Just tell me… you can talk to me about anything!" Keith told Whitney that he knew they were getting closer each day with intense feelings for each other. He mentioned how fast things were moving between them and wanted to share something with her before things got out of hand. He then disclosed to Whitney of his home *situation*. He told her of the unhappiness in his marriage but his love for KJ… and about his wife Amanda being pregnant with a baby that may not be his. All of a sudden, Whitney's facial expression completely changed! It was as if she was becoming nauseated and throw-up over the table at any minute. Then she removed her hand from Keith's grip and refused to look at him.

The once loving and flirtatious couple in the restaurant was now looking as if they were an old married couple on the fence of an argument. She turned back to Keith and asked why he wait so long to tell her about him being married. She wished that he had told her that when he first met her. She questioned why he would wait until she was falling for him to drop this by-the-way-I'm-married bomb on her? It was so quiet at the dining table. No one said a word for what seemed like eternity. The once sweet aroma of love and lust was now tainted with heartbreak, embarrassment and hurt. Keith tried to reach over and hug Whitney but she brushed him off with a cold shoulder.

Seeing Whitney was about to start crying, Keith motioned to the waiter and asked him for the check. After paying for the meals, they grabbed their belongings and walked out of the restaurant. While walking towards his car, Keith tried to hold Whitney's hand but she jerked her hand away from him. When they got to the car, Keith unlocked it with the remote and walked over to open the passenger's door for Whitney. Before he could get around to her side of the car, she looked at him as though she could *kill* him and said, "I can open the door myself, just take me home!"

Keith raised both his hands and backed away from the door. Even he knew that when a woman is upset, it's *best* to give her space. As they both sat in the car, sniffles echoed from Whitney who tried her best to hold-in her emotions. Keith tried again to reach over and grab her hand but she refused to let him touch her. Whitney then begged Keith to take her home. It was a forty-five-minute ride back to

Raleigh and for the entire forty-five minutes, Whitney said absolutely nothing to Keith.

This was not how Keith had planned his life to be when he got married. He never thought he would say "I DO" and then question the trust in his marriage. He never thought that he would have thoughts of divorce. He never imagined that he would ever have to question the paternity of their unborn child. Now he's out with *another* woman who was starting to love him and now he has hurt her too. He never expected that he and Whitney would get so close to each other…so fast. He figured they would get together for sex a few times and that would be it, nothing more than that.

When they arrived at her parents' home, she looked over at Keith with a face full of tears. She had cried so much until the mascara under her eyelid ran down her cheeks from Keith's confession. She opened the car door and let herself out. He helplessly watched her as she walked towards the door of her parents' home. Whitney didn't call or text Keith for a week. She didn't reply to his phone call nor his text messages either. The last thing Keith wanted to do was to hurt *another* person. He knew that the truth might cause Whitney to never speak to him again but he needed to let her know the truth, even if it hurts.

21

RED LIGHT SPECIAL

Keith knew he had to make it up to Whitney somehow. He had hurt her to the core with his confession. Maybe he should have told her sooner than he did about it. He knew that it wasn't fair to her to expect a long-term relationship with him with knowing the details. Regardless of the situation, Keith and Whitney had gotten pretty close in a way that felt more than just physical. They had chemistry and they both knew it. There were times when she and Keith would text each other at the same time or call simultaneously as the other person was thinking of them. It's hard to find someone like that.

The Monday prior to Valentine's Day, Keith was working dayshift and was at the end of his shift. While on the way home, he thought of Whitney. He thought of the fun conversations they had shared with each other over the past few weeks. He was wondering how she was doing and hoping that she was still there with her folks. While he thought about her, a text alert came across his phone. It was Whitney! It was as if she had telepathically felt him thinking about her. She explained how much she had missed him and wanted to see him. She apologized for being very judgmental initially. Keith was so surprised at the text but was also happy to hear from her. He asked if she was busy and if he could stop by for a few minutes. She said she wasn't busy and that she wanted to see him too… if he had a moment.

Keith made a detour and traveled to visit Whitney. When he arrived, she was standing outside the car garage. When the two embraced each other, it was as though they hadn't seen each other in at least a year. She really missed Keith and he missed her too. It was getting close to Valentine's Day. Things at Keith's home were still the same with uncertainty and lack of affection. Desperate for affection and attention, Keith decided to make it up to Whitney. He told Whitney of his plans to make arrangements for them to spend the night together on Valentine's Day. Realizing how cold his marriage had become, Keith didn't think twice before reserving the room at the hotel. He waited until Amanda left to visit a friend and used her laptop to book the room at a very nice hotel. Things were all set. When Amanda returned, he her that he wanted to hanging out with some co-workers on Friday night.

When Friday came, instead of enjoying an innocent evening with co-workers, Keith picked Whitney up and took her out to eat at a very nice hibachi restaurant outside of Durham called Akashi. They ate and laughed in each other's presence just as they did on their first date. Since Keith had put it all on the table about his situation, he felt relieved and free to talk with Whitney about any and everything. They enjoyed a wonderful meal that was prepared by the hibachi chef and took turns feeding each other from their plate.

They both enjoyed a glass of Moscato wine while exchanging kisses that seemed to intensify with every touch of their lips. Whitney and Keith were getting lost in the heat of passion with their raging hormones. The two knew that this would be the night they finally get to explore one another in a way they had imagined since day one of their flirting. It didn't matter that it was Valentine's Day for the two; things were *already* steamy from their long anticipation. When they were finished eating, Whitney even offered to pay for the meal but Keith thanked her and paid for it. They walked out of the restaurant and traveled to their hotel for the night. Keith had booked the room at one of the nicer hotels in Durham, the DoubleTree by Hilton.

They stopped by the wine store and got another bottle of Moscato, some chocolate and some candles. Keith really wanted to make the night memorable for the two.

When they arrived at the hotel, Keith and Whitney checked in and made their way up to their suite. They kissed from the time they entered the elevator until they entered the room. Once they entered the room, Whitney asked if it would be okay to take a shower before getting relaxed. Keith prepared the room while she started the shower. While in the shower, Keith laid the rose pedals all over the floor. There was a trail of rose pedals that led from the bathroom door to the bed where a plate of chocolates, a chilled bottle of wine, and two glasses were in place. Keith prepared the setting within three minutes. After choosing R. Kelly's channel on Pandora, Keith decided to join Whitney in the shower. He quickly took of his clothes and walked into the bathroom. The steam greeted him at the door. He walked in and saw Whitney's silhouette through the glass shower.

Keith walked into the shower with Whitney and began to kiss her on the back of her neck then down her shoulders. She leaned her head to the side while feeling the sensations of Keith's kisses permeate every nerve-ending. Whitney didn't care about getting her hair wet. She had the kind of hair that curled at the hint of heat or water.

With her long, wet, curly hair running down the middle of her back, Keith turned her around and started kissing Whitney on her lips then down her neck. He kissed her body while the mixture of water and her perfume ran across his tongue. He caressed her waist and kissed her lower neck as the water ran down his waves and his sparkling earrings. Keith squeezed Whitney closer to him as he started sucking and licking all over her right breast. Whitney began to moan as the licking of her nipple sent arousing sensations down towards her throbbing clit. She rubbed his head as he licked and slid his tongue over to suck her left nipple. Keith's cock was now like a rocket standing straight up and ready to go into outer space.

He spun Whitney around and made her place both palms against the wall facing the shower head. She arched her back as the hot water ran down her back and down her butt cheeks. Keith grabbed her small twenty-four inch waist as she arched her back even more in anticipation of him sliding into her universe. Keith placed his left hand on Whitney's left shoulder and grabbed his dick with his right hand. He slid his manhood across her soft ass but just before his cock met her vaginal opening...Whitney turned around and said, "Nah, not yet...let's wait until after the shower. You remember that night in your patrol car you stopped me when you knew I wanted it? Karma is a bitch right?" She said those words as sexy as she could while laughing and walking out of the shower to dry off. "Oh... I see it's like that huh? Hmmm, okay you got me back! But shhh-hiiiitt!" Said Keith who stood there with a hard dick and a funny smirk on his face.

While the two were in the shower, Amanda decided to call Keith to make sure he was okay and to let him know that she was about to go to bed for the night. KJ was asleep and the house was very quiet. All that was left was her husband being by her side. The phone rang but no answer from Keith. She tried two more times but still no answer. She left a voicemail on his phone and figured he was in a noisy place and couldn't hear his phone ringing.

Keith turned off the shower. They both dried themselves off and walked out of the bathroom. As Whitney wrapped her wet hair in a towel in an Erica Badu style, she looked down and the trail of rose pedals on the floor that led to the bed, the chocolates, and the wine. She covered her mouth in amazement! "How did you... when did you do this?" "Doesn't matter when or how I did it... the question is, do you like it?" asked Keith while embracing Whitney from behind and kissing her on her neck. "Yes, I do Keith! No one has ever done this for me. Usually men just do things they think make me happy. But you did this from your heart baby...thank you!" Whitney's eyes started to fill with tears. "Okay...don't go crying on me! Have a seat and let me pour you a glass of wine. Whitney walked over and sat on the soft couch while Keith poured them a glass of wine.

As Keith picked up his cell phone to change the channel on Pandora, he saw the missed calls from Amanda. To prevent any *further* interruptions, he switched his phone to silent mode and placed his phone upside down on the table near the kitchen of the suite. The temperature in the room was warm and just right for romance. Keith handed Whitney the glass of wine and sat next to her. The two ate a few pieces of chocolate and chatted while Pandora's playlist seemed to be aligned with their sexual energy. The station was playing all of the right songs to woo the couple of the night. They started kissed each other as the song "The Love Scene" by the artist Joe played softly in the background. Keith and Whitney were ready to create ecstasy.

The room was completely dark with only the quiet illumination of the candles that reflected off the shiny dilated pupils of their eyes. Keith began to slowly kiss Whitney as they both stood by the edge of the bed. This was what they both had been waiting for so long. He kissed her gently on the lips while running his hands towards the knot on the towel that kept her covered. Just as his hand reached the knot, Whitney stopped him. She stood up, grabbed Keith by the hand and led him towards the foot of the bed. She made him sit on the bed facing her then she whispered in his ear, "let me please you... and don't tell me no!" Keith wasn't used to this, he was ALWAYS in the driver's seat but tonight he was about to ride shotgun in the passenger's seat. As he sat on the foot of the bed, Whitney leaned forward and began to kiss him. Her body language was so seductive as if she was telling Keith that he was going to be her *bitch* tonight!

Every soft kiss from her was full of passion and energy. She could immediately tell from her kisses that it had been a long time since he had been kissed in that way. She could tell that he had not been genuinely pleased in that way in a long time. Whitney kissed Keith's lips and licked all around them as she moved down his neck towards his collarbone. Keith did his best to resist the urge to jump back in the driver's seat. She kissed his collarbone and slid her wet and warm tongue down his chest. She kissed and licked his tattoos and then his nipples. She began doing mini circles all around it causing Keith to moan at her talent. After kissing, licking, and gently biting his upper body, Whitney kept licking and kissing down towards his belly button. The smell of Keith's cologne was still engraved in his skin and it filled her nose. She licked the creases of his abdominal muscle then down passed his belly button. Keith's heart rate was beginning to speed up as he leaned forward.

When Keith leaned forward, Whitney abruptly pushed him back to lay down with her hand. As she prepared herself to pleasure him, she slowly kissed down towards his shaved cock. As she kissed around the base of his manhood, she could literally see the veins on his cock pumped with blood and the head of if throbbing from her kisses, as she got closer to it. Whitney was in charge and she wanted him to know it. She leaned her head forward with no hands, opened her mouth, and stuck her tongue out and vertically gently licked his chocolate shaft. After a few licks, Whitney drew the head of his cock with her mouth like a suction. As Silk's song "If You" played in the background, she began stroking his endowed shaft with her right hand while slowly sucking the head of his cock. Keith could not believe how good she was at pleasing him!

With her wet and warm tongue, she licked the right side of his shaft. She even went lower and slowly licked his scrotum while stroking his dick up and down steadily with both of her hands. Whitney stroked his endowed cock faster and faster causing Keith to raise his torso off the bed from the erotic pleasures. She made him lay back again then took the liberty to lick the head of his dick one last time then rose to her feet and straddled him facing away from him (reverse cowgirl position). She reached back, grabbed his dick with one hand and placed it at her vaginal opening. Once it was inside, she slowly rode his dick while the candle light glistened on his manhood from her wetness. Whitney slowly rode Keith's endowed manhood while she breathed deeply to take all of him. She rode him halfway and slow at first. Then her rhythm increased as her feminine dam broke enabling her to ride him faster while Keith palmed her soft ass with his massive hands.

※

By this time, Amanda became a little worried. She couldn't sleep and really wanted to hear from her husband. She called two more times but no answer. Realizing that she might be up for a while from worrying, she decided to log onto her *laptop* to do some work for her job.

Meanwhile, Whitney was finally intimate with her new sexual encounter. She began to think of the first encounter with him and the first conversation in his patrol car. She thought of the fact that she was literally *fucking the law* and it felt so good to have him in her life. She began to breath deeper and Keith's cock seemed to fill every space within her feminine universe. She began to moan deeper as she reached closer to her climax. When she could no longer hold it in, she moaned and gritted her bottom lip with her teeth then violently released her *love* all over him. She slowed her grind motion indicating her release. Keith, realizing that she had climax, picked Whitney up and stood with his manhood still in her. He then rotated her around so that she was facing him. He gently laid her on her back into the missionary position and entered her by stroking faster and deeper. After a few minutes in that position, he was already close to climaxing; Whitney begged him to cum *inside* her! Keith looked at her with discontent and slowed his rhythm. "I just came off of my cycle two days ago…you got the green light to cum in me! I want it inside me baby!" After locking her ankles behind Keith's back, he sped up his rhythm again then exploded inside of her! The two cuddled then fell asleep while listening to Pandora's love songs. That would be one of almost three sessions that night.

22

CAUGHT UP

The next morning, Keith went downstairs to get breakfast for Whitney and himself. While he was away, the telephone in their hotel room rang. Whitney was very hesitant to answer it but figured it was Keith on the other end. Maybe he wanted to know what kind of food to bring back to the room. Wrapped in only a white bed sheet, Whitney slowly arose from the bed to answer the telephone. Still naked from the night before, she answered the phone. "Hello..." she said.

"Is this Whitney?" a *female* voice asked abruptly!

"Yes...why? Who is this?" answered Whitney surprisingly.

"This is Keith's *wife*, just tell him that his son KJ is asking for him and wanted to know when he is coming home to us?" yelled the female on the other end! The phone call ended abruptly in a *forceful* hang up leaving Whitney with the telephone shaking in her hand. *It was Amanda!*

Whitney could not believe what just happened. She broke down and started crying on the floor. All she could think about was the fact that Amanda not only discovered that Keith was cheating, but she also knew where they were and now she knows her name! She felt like a total home wrecker.

When Keith returned to the room, he returned with a tray full of food. He walked inside the room with a huge smile on his face hoping to find Whitney excited to see him. Instead, he entered the room only to discover the countenance on Whitney's face as if she had seen a ghost. The gleam that was once in Whitney's eyes was now full of despondency and despair. Keith could immediately tell that something wasn't right! "Are you okay? What's wrong baby?" asked Keith. Whitney sadly looked at Keith and said, "your wife called…she said you need to come home!" The look on her face told Keith that she was scared as hell. "Did, she call my cell phone? Why would you even answer it when you saw her name on the caller ID? Hell, why would you even answer my phone period?" Asked Keith. "…she didn't call your cell phone Keith!" answered Whitney while looking at the phone belonging to the room. Keith's facial expression told Whitney just how shocked he was at the news. "How did Amanda know I'm here?" Keith silently asked himself. He immediately backtracked everywhere they were the night before. He didn't remember seeing anyone that knew him at the restaurant or in the hotel. Keith tried to play it off as if everything was okay, but even he knew that things were about to get crazy! "Keith, she knows my name!" yelled Whitney.

Shit just got real for Keith, Whitney, and Amanda. "I'm sorry baby... I'll handle it!" said Keith with confidence. The two packed their belongings without even eating breakfast and returned to Raleigh. Keith and Whitney said nothing to each other all the way to Whitney's parent's home. That ride seemed like the longest ride in Keith's life. His heart and mind were racing. His palms were sweaty and his stomach felt like it was in a twisted knot.

A half an hour passed, Keith finally arrived at Whitney's parent's home. Keith began pleading with Whitney that everything would be okay but she exited his car as if his words were just a soft echo. Keith watched her open the door of her parents' home then backed out of the driveway. He was now on his way to his house. Keith wasn't sure what to expect when he got home. Would his belongings be tossed out into the front lawn? Will Amanda be standing in the front door when he arrived? He silently prayed all the way home.

He arrived home. Keith opened the door and saw Amanda in the kitchen feeding KJ. It took no time at all for Amanda to start fussing at Keith. She started fussing at him for sneaking off to a hotel to be with another woman? Most importantly, why would he do that to her while she's pregnant with his child? Keith immediately started fussing back at her. All the anger he had built up within him exploded!

"Amanda, how could you even ask me that question when the baby that you're carrying may not even be mine? All this mistrust with texts and pictures in your phone and emails from all these dudes made me so upset with this whole situation. So yeah, I went to the hotel with her! You were doing your thing so *why* couldn't I?" said Keith while shedding tears. The tears flowed uncontrollably down Keith's face. Amanda had never seen Keith cry before… ever. He then looked over at KJ who had stopped eating and was now staring at him. "Daddy, you crying?" Keith then covered his face and went into the guest room. He shut the door and sat on the bed trying to compose himself. Keith knew that what he had done was wrong on so many levels. Whether he was caught or not, he knew it was wrong! However, what he couldn't understand was how Amanda could jump all over him when he suspected that she had done the same thing to him? The only difference between him and Amanda was the fact that she didn't get caught up like he did. He never tell a soul about her alleged infidelity.

After about thirty minutes passed, what happened next took Keith by surprise. Amanda knocked on the door where he was, came in and sat next to him on the bed. *She apologized to Keith!* Amanda seemed to have heard Keith's thoughts telepathically. She said she was apologizing because with all that they were going through with mistrust, she understood why he would do what he did. Not that it was right, but she was apologizing, as if it was *her* fault, that Keith cheated. She explained to him how she found out. When Keith reserved the room, he used her laptop and forgot to close the window. So, when she logged on that morning to do work, she saw the reservation of the hotel on her laptop. The two kissed and hugged each other. They sat and held each other's hand. Each one apologizing to the other from their heart. They decided to try counseling with Amanda's pastor again to rebuild their troubled home.

23

CRAZY IN LOVE

What Keith didn't realize was that Whitney had broken up with a lawyer, before meeting him, who had hurt her heart to the core. She had vowed not to get sexually involved with another man until she was engaged or married. But somehow, she let her guard down with Keith. Even though she was being very flirtatious by sending him naked photos, freaky texts and phone calls whenever time permitted, she was still heartbroken from the lawyer. When she returned home from the unfortunate ending of their romantic getaway during Valentine's Day weekend, she cried herself to sleep. She didn't speak to anyone for the rest of that night. She didn't leave home for the next three days. Whitney was refusing to bathe, eat, or groom herself because of the situation she found herself in with Keith. Her parents were becoming concerned with Whitney. What Keith didn't know was that Whitney was diagnosed with bipolar disorder. Her parents were becoming more and more worried because the last episode started after a traumatic event two year ago.

On the fourth day of being stuck in the house, Whitney opened her bedroom door and went downstairs to get something to eat. Her parents were backing out of the driveway. They left her a note to let her know that they were going to the store but would be back shortly. After reading the note, Whitney went to find her cell phone. She had no missed calls or texts from Keith. Not even a DM message from him.

Whitney went on Instagram and saw that Keith had updated photos of him looking happy to be with his family. Whitney became irate! She was upset that he could post updates on social media but couldn't text or call her! She then clicked on his profile picture and began to stare at it. She stared at his photo for one minute without *even* moving her head. Keith had been the first person she slept with since the breakup of her last boyfriend and she was *not* about to let him go that easily.

Whitney went to Keith's Instagram page and "liked" every single photo he had ever posted. Every picture in every album was "liked" by her! She went and "liked" every status that he had posted on Facebook. Then Whitney updated her Facebook status by telling everyone that she was now in *love*! Since she had a huge following, it took no time for her to be questioned by her friends as to "who" she was madly in love with, but she didn't comment as to who it was.

The following day, Amanda had a taste for some strawberry ice cream, pickles, peanut butter, and Oreos. Her pregnancy craving kept Keith laughing at her. It was getting late in the evening and was dark outside. Since KJ was sleeping, she asked Keith to get them. He drove to the local Walmart and found all the items that he needed from there. After checking out, he walked to his car and noticed a car that was backed under a tree facing him. He got into his car and drove off. As he approached the traffic light from the store, he noticed that the same car was now following him. Instead of making a left turn to go towards his home, Keith's trooper instincts kicked in and he made a right turn. The car also made a right turn behind him. When he would switch lanes, the car would switch lanes too. Keith knew that he was definitely being followed now. Since he was a trooper, Keith never left home without his backup weapon on him. He pulled into a nearby gas station and the car up pulled next to him. Keith grabbed his gun to prepare to protect his life but then… the car looked familiar. It was Whitney!

She rolled her window and partially smiled at Keith. He was furious! She could have been shot for real! However, when she rolled her window down, Keith saw her appearance. Whitney hadn't combed her hair and was wearing an old dingy-wrinkled white t-shirt with brown sweat pants. Keith got out of his car and walked over to the driver's side door. Whitney rolled down the window and said, "Hey baby! I really miss you!" Keith could smell her odor as soon as she let the window down. She hadn't bathe in days and she definitely smelled like it!

"What are you doing Whitney? Why the hell were you following me like that? You're lucky you didn't get shot just now!" said Keith. "I know, but I just wanted to see you baby. I figured I could just follow you until you stopped somewhere. I really miss you Keith!" she said. Whitney began explaining to Keith that she missed him and wanted to be with him. After about five minutes of talking with her, Keith said, "Listen, it was good seeing you Whitney but I gotta go! I'll catch up with you soon!" He walked over and got back into his car. But before he could leave, she motioned for him to roll his window down. Keith rolled his window down and looked at Whitney. She looked at Keith, with her hair dangling all over the place, and said, "I-love-you Keith!" Then she blew a kiss into his direction. She waited for Keith to reply. By this time, Keith is so caught off guard. He thought about switching his car into reverse and spinning off at the sound of the l-word.

But while looking in Whitney's direction, he could see her eyes getting bigger and tears flowing down her cheeks. Keith hated to see any woman cry, especially over him.

He looked once again in her direction and said, "I love you too… good night!" To Keith they were *just words* but to Whitney, his words were life! Keith left and returned home.

Weeks passed and Amanda had their second son. It was a beautiful baby boy. The paternity test came back with Keith being 99.9% the father. Keith was back to doing well on his job with the highway patrol. KJ was enjoying daycare and they were all happy to have the new edition, baby Julian, home with them. One day Keith and Amanda were at home enjoying the day off from work. They usually don't get the same days off but Keith had some comp days from work. The two had just finished having sex in the den while a movie was playing in the background. After the movie ended, Amanda decided to go take a quick shower and fix her hair while KJ was at daycare. While she was walking towards the master bathroom, someone ranged the doorbell. Keith told Amanda to go ahead and take a shower. He told her that he would answer the door then come jump in the shower with her. He spanked her on the ass as she walked towards the bedroom.

Keith walked up to the door and opened it. When he opened the door, he was shocked to see who was standing there in his doorway! It was Whitney! She stood wearing a long brown leather coat with fierce red heels. Whitney knows where he lives! With a straight-face he asked Whitney, "What the *fuck* are you doing here? How did you know where I live?" This he said as he closed the door behind him to cancel any chances of Amanda hearing him yelling. Whitney replied, "But baby I missed you so much! I just had to find you to let you know that I haven't been the same since you left me. That night at the hotel was so special to me. I understand your hurt and unhappiness with your marriage. I can make you happy, I promise! I love you so much Keith! You're supposed to be my husband baby!" said Whitney as she rubbed the right side of Keith's face. After pushing her hand away from his face, she opened her leather jacket and there she stood completely NAKED! No bra, no panties, and no hair on her pussy! NAKED!

Keith took one look at her tanned skin with chiseled abs and almost forgot where he was temporarily. His mind immediately flashed back to the night at the hotel. Her pussy felt so good while he was stroking it. He didn't wear a condom which made the flashback more intense. It was so tight and stayed wet no matter how long Keith took to climax. They were intimate almost three times that night. It was *almost* three because he couldn't get another erection on the third attempt during their sex marathon.

It was almost as if she was trying to *seduce* him right there in his own nest! "Whitney, you have to go!" said Keith pushing her away from the door! "But Keith...baby, you're supposed to be my husband...I-I had visited a psychic and had my palm read and everything! Keith, you are the one!" said Whitney. "Bitch, get the fuck outta her with that shit!" yelled Keith while pointing towards her car. Whitney walked to her car and turned on the ignition and starting backing up to leave.

After backing, she placed the car in drive then stopped in the middle of the neighborhood roadway. She looked into the direction of Keith who was still standing outside the doorway and gave him a stare that would *kill* as she sped away. Keith knew that look from anywhere. He knew he would have to deal with her again. Just as he went back into the house and closed the door, Amanda walked into the living room still drying her hair with a towel. "What took you so long? And who was that anyway?" asked Amanda while wearing nothing but a towel. "Oh, that was just the neighbor; he wanted to know if I could help him with a ticket for a family member, that's all. Damn, look at your fine ass! Come here woman!" said Keith as he began chasing Amanda throughout the house!

24

THE SET UP

It was the weekend before Labor Day and Keith was off for three days: Friday, Saturday, and Sunday. That Saturday, Amanda was on call and had to go take care of a patient while Keith stayed home with the boys. While she was away, Keith thought it would be a great idea to have a daddy and sons day. He fed the boys, cleaned them up, and got them dressed to head out. All three of the men wore red golf shirts and khaki shorts with black and red Jordan shoes.

Keith loved spending time with his boys. This would be another day at the park along with, maybe having ice cream, afterwards to finish the day. They finally made their way to a neighborhood park ten minutes from their home. The park was very close to Amanda's job. Keith held Julian while KJ enjoyed the playing with other kids on slides and other fun things in the park. Then he placed KJ and Julian in a safety swing so that they both could swing together. Keith was enjoying the moment more than KJ and Julian. He was always very vocal with his excitement when playing with his sons. The other parents were pretty used to his bubbly expressions.

Keith gave his boys a huge push on the swing then reached for his cell phone. He wanted to capture this moment on video with his phone to share with Amanda and social media. While videoing the boys playing in the swing, Keith noticed Whitney's car pull up behind his parked car. "Ahhh shhiittt!" whispered Keith. "Ahhh-Shiiit!' Said KJ, repeating his father's words. "KJ! Don't say that word again okay? That's a word for adults! Understand?" replied Keith. "Okay daddy, I understand!"

Whitney rolled down her window and waved at Keith. He nonchalantly waved back. Keith stood there silently praying that she would leave *considering* he was busy spending quality time with the boys. Instead of leaving, Whitney opened the car door and walked towards him. She was wearing a black NY Yankee fitted hat, blue daisy-dukes jeans, black five inch heels, and a white cut-off t-shirt to show her abs. Whitney was walking like she was on the runway towards Keith. As she walked towards him like Beyoncé in a music video, a loud *slap* echoed next to Keith. A wife had slapped her husband for staring intensely at Whitney ass!

She walked toward Keith and yelled. "Hi Keith!" Keith knew he better play it off quickly while the other parents looked at her with disgrace. "What's up fam?" Keith said while giving Whitney a "church-hug" (family-like hug).

"What are you doing here?" quietly asked Keith as he focused back to pushing the boys on the swing. "Who is that daddy?" asked KJ. "I was thinking about you so much lately. I was just in the area and saw your car. I figured I'd stop by to say hello!" she replied. "Oh okay! Good to see you, now can you please go? You know I'm still married! Someone here might know my wife! Please… just go!" demanded Keith. "I will do as you say, but Keith do you have an extra wet wipe?" asked Whitney. "A wet wipe? Why the hell do you need a wet wipe for? Keith asked while trying to look civil. "Well baby, I was thinking about the last time I sucked your big ass cock and how good it felt when I *cam* all—over---it. Then I thought of how hard your dick was when you *cam* inside me! Now…I need a wet wipe because…my pussy is *wet*… that's all!"

Keith shook his head and tried his best to ignore Whitney. His cell phone vibrated. It was Amanda! She text his phone to know where he and the boys were so that she could meet them. Keith text her back that they were at the park and were getting ready to come home shortly. Amanda insisted on meeting them at the park. So, she was on her way. "Whitney, my wife is on the way here… please go!" whispered Keith. "Okay, see me tonight please! I'll be waiting!" said Whitney as she slowly walked away towards her car. She waved and left. Another slap echoed in Keith's ear. The same woman slapped her husband again for staring at Whitney's ass while she walked away! She left.

In less than five minutes, Amanda showed up to the playground as the boys were being fasten in their seatbelt in the car. She greeted them all with a kiss then they all headed home. Keith followed Amanda while she drove her car. What a close call for Keith! Having the two women publicly meet was not what he needed! That evening, Whitney was all that Keith could think about. He hadn't thought of her like this in a long time. He had really missed their conversations. Their conversations were always enlightening and full of energy.

That same evening, Keith's neighbor from next door, Mr. Jamison, visited their home. Mr. Jamison was known to be a heavy alcohol drinker. He had been out the night before and was too inebriated to drive back home. Mr. Jamison was a husband and a father of five children.

He was in his late sixties, short, plump and had a Mike Tyson kind of voice. Even though he was Caucasian, he was married to a black woman for over forty years. He was more down-to-earth than anyone Keith knew in their small neighborhood. He was a very nice but nosey neighbor. He always dressed as though he was about to go to church. He would wear a nice pair of slacks, a collared plaid shirt, a black kangol hat, suspenders and church shoes with no socks.

On this evening, Mr. Jamison stopped by and asked Amanda if Keith could take him to his brother's house so that he could pick up his car that he left over there. Mr. Jamison's brother had already gone to work for the evening and Mrs. Jamison had been fussing at him to go get the car. After making Amanda and Keith laugh at his story, Amanda agreed that Keith should help him. KJ and Julian were about to take a bath from playing at the park earlier. Amanda realized that by the time Keith got back, the boys would be asleep and they could have some *quality* time together. Keith kissed his family goodbye and walked with Mr. Jamison to get into his car. KJ and Julian waved at their dad while the two men backed out of the driveway. Amanda gave a final wave then shut the mahogany door.

As soon as they were and out of sight from the house, Mr. Jamison, in his Mike Tyson voice looked over and yelled at Keith, "You ever get tir'd of being married Keith? I *know* you gotta be tir'd too! My wife just nags and nags my ass to death every night man! Baby do this and baby could you do that…boy, I swear Keith, I'm sick and tir'd of it myself. I know what I needs ta'do, needs to gon'head and get me an ole *sidepiece!* You know, a nice tall ass amazon woman like da one you had come over to yo' house that time!" Keith looked at Mr. Jamison as though he had seen a *ghost* then quickly looked back onto the highway.

"Didn't think I saw her that day she showed up at yo' house in that long trench coat huh? She been naked up under that coat ain't-it' bo?" Keith shook his head while smiling and quietly said, "yeah, she was…I was hoping nobody saw her that day! Where were you at? I didn't see you in your yard…" Mr. Jamison leaned over towards Keith and told him that he had seen her when she pulled into the driveway through his bathroom window. "Keith, listen, I know e'erthing that goes on in my neighborhood. I might *act* like I ain't got no sense, but I sees' everything! Look at me…e'erthing! Like that night you cried like a lil' *bitch* in your car! (Laughs at Keith) But anyway bo, like I said, yeah when I saw that car pull up in yo' driveway and that tall pretty amazon stepped outta that car…and had on dem' heels and that trench coat. When I saw her bo, I said oooh'shiiiiiit! But Keith, you did good by keeping yo' composure. Just be glad Gladys (his wife) ain't see you wit' her! Lord she would've been dialing yalls' house number and all!" Then Keith replied, "Okay, you got me Mr. Jamison, keep that between you and me please! Where are we going anyway?"

SEDUCTION

Mr. Jamison pointed Keith in the location where his car was located. To Keith's surprise, it was on the same street as Whitney's parents' house. As they passed Whitney's parents' home, Keith looked over and saw Whitney's car parked in the driveway. "It was tha' same car that was at yo' house? Sho'l is Keith!" Yelled Mr. Jamison while looking over Keith's shoulder. "Bo, is you hav'n relations that girl who lives ova'there? Oh my God Keith, if that's who I think it is, I know her folks. Bo, she is fine like primetime son! I heard she kinda crazy though but God *knows* I's still hit it!" chucked Mr. Jamison.

❧

Finally, Mr. Jamison and Keith made it to his car. He dropped him off and made sure Mr. Jamison's car cranked before leaving him. Then they both backed out of the driveway. Keith allowed Mr. Jamison leave first then he followed behind. Keith slowed his speed down to let Mr. Jamison get ahead then he made a right turn into Whitney's parents' driveway. Keith hadn't been there in a long time. He called Whitney's phone but she didn't answer. Realizing that he probably shouldn't be there anyway, he got nervous and decided to leave while he could. But before he completely backed out of the driveway, Whitney called him back. He told her that he was in her neighborhood and just wanted to stop by to say *hello*. She asked him if he could come in for a few minutes to chat? Keith figured a short visit to say *hello* shouldn't hurt.

He parked his car and walked up to the door in the garage. He noticed that her parents' car was gone. Their car was always parked in the garage. As he got to the door, Whitney opened the door wearing only a bath towel. "I was in the shower, that's why I missed your call baby! Come in..." While looking at her countenance, he could tell that she was crying earlier. "Look Whitney, if this is a bad time I understand. I just wanted to say hey...that's all!" Said Keith, as he stood in the doorway hesitant to go inside the home. "No no, it's okay Keith, my parents just left to go grocery shopping. Mom is making a huge dinner for our family tomorrow so they will be at the store for a while. I was crying so hard right before you came though."

Keith walked in and closed the door behind him. He stood a few feet away from the door. "What were you crying about?" he asked with a serious look on his face. "Keith, I am so jealous!" "Jealous? Jealous of what?" After a few sniffles, she said, "I'm jealous because your wife his *something* from you that I don't have?" "Something like what?" "Well, she has two sons from you and well...I don't have anything like *that* from you Keith." Cried Whitney while walking towards the laundry room. Keith thought of how weird it was for her to be jealous of the fact that he had sons with Amanda and not considered their *short-lived* love affair.

As she continued to cry, Keith walked over and gave her a small hug. His plan was to console her from crying for a few seconds then leave. The last thing he wanted to do was to give her any signs that he felt sorry for her *strange* reason for being jealous so he attempted to release the hug. As he tried to release her, Whitney leaned in and hugged him tighter. Whitney hadn't felt Keith's body and quite a while. She loved the smell of his cologne. "I miss you so much baby. Please hug me..." Keith, still ready to leave before things get way out of hand, leaned in and hugged her tighter. Whitney sniffed and wiped her tears with her hands but when the tears continued to flow, she did the next best thing. She backed away from Keith slightly and *removed* her towel to dry her tears. Keith knew he had better go quickly now but Whitney was crying. The last thing he wanted was for her parents to return home to see her crying with him in their home with her completely naked. "Whitney, please stop crying... please!" Whitney looked up at Keith and dropped the towel from her hands. As the towel hit the floor, there she stood completely naked. She looked up at Keith, leaned forward and kissed him slowly on his lips.

꧂

Feeling that Keith was trying to leave; she hopped on the dryer, spread her legs and used her fingers to open the doors to her heated universe. Like a *serpent* advertising a delicious red apple, she leaned back and begged Keith to fuck her. She told him that his cock was the only *thing* that could make her *feel* better! Keith looked at the golden skin of Whitney's body. He quickly scanned her titties and sculpted abs that were all covered with baby oil as she sat on the dryer with her legs spread wide opened. Knowing that her parents would be back soon, he said, "Whitney, I can't do this! Plus, your parents will be back in a minute…and I…" "Keith, they will be gone for at least another thirty minutes. Plus, I can see them when they pull up into the driveway from here. So baby please, give me that dick!" Keith hesitated, then took a deep breath and slowly removed his belt. His pants dropped to the floor. He moved in closer to her body until his hips met the inside of her thighs. Whitney placed a small amount of spit on her fingers. She then reached down, grabbed his endowed manhood and guided the head to her opening. As soon as the head of his cock met her vaginal opening, Whitney was full of excitement as it gently slid inside. After a few mini-strokes, he was able to slide inside her without hesitation. He reached around and palmed her ass while he fucked her slowly on the dryer.

After only a few minutes, Whitney *climaxed* all over his manhood from her intense love for Keith. After she *climaxed*, she asked Keith to back up a little. She then climbed down the dryer, bent over and leans against the dryer, with her elbows, for doggy style access for Keith. She spread her legs while Keith entered her from behind. Keith looked down at her golden backside and long black curly hair as he guided his dick back inside her wet universe. He started giving Whitney every inch she could take while holding on to her right shoulder with his right hand and the other

SEDUCTION

hand caressed her waist. He could hear her *cum* fall to the floor, Keith was now ready to *climax.*

Whitney was *very* aware of the *time of month* for her cycle to start and end. When Keith *cam* in her that night in the hotel room, her cycle had just ended. She had Keith complete trust in her. She didn't miss any cycles the following months either. As Keith was nearing his climax, Whitney moaned, "you got the *green light* baby... *cum* hard in me please! I want it inside me Keith! Fill me up please baby!"

Moments later, Keith *violently released* inside her then leaned over to rest his head momentarily on her back. Keith hadn't climaxed that hard in a long time. After feeling Keith's climax hit her cervix, Whitney turned around and kissed him. While kissing her, Keith saw a book on the corner of the laundry room that was entitled "How to Seduce the Man of Your Dreams". Then it hit Keith what had happen! Whitney's crying was just an act. It was just a way to get him to stay longer and have sex with her. He quickly got dressed. Seeing the bathroom just outside the laundry room, Keith rushed into it to wash away the *smell* of sex. He knew he had to get rid of the scent of sex before going home to Amanda. Whitney stood at the door of the laundry room naked and smiled at Keith who was busy cleaning himself off. She could see him while looking through the door of the bathroom that was ajar.

As soon as he finished drying off, he opened the door slightly. He took one last look at the mirror to make sure his clothes were arranged, then walked out. Keith looked over and saw Whitney standing there naked with a smile still on her face. "Thank you for that baby! That was just what I needed. I feel so much better now!" said Whitney. "Yeah, I bet." replied Keith while walking towards the door. He opened the door and let himself out. He cranked up his car and exited her driveway as quickly as possible. Before he could get to the stop sign at the end of the road, Whitney's parents turned down the residential road passing Keith. That was a close call! Minutes later, Keith arrived home. Amanda was sitting in the den on the phone talking to her sorority sister from Tampa. They were talking about their upcoming retreat. The boys were already in the bed for the night. When Amanda saw Keith enter the house, she looked at him and said, "Ahh sir, go straight to the shower please and thank you!" Keith's heart seemed to had skipped a beat! He began to think the worse as to why she would say that to him. "What do you mean, go straight to the shower?" Asked Keith for clarification. "Mr. Jamison stopped by about thirty minutes ago to thank me for letting you help him. He said you were driving behind him but you stopped to help some old ladies change their flat tire down the road. He said he told you that he would let me know. Now go take a shower 'cause I don't wanna smell that dirt on you! Anyway, child I can't wait to go down to Florida…." Amanda continued her conversation as Keith made his way to take the shower. Mr. Jamison must have seen him make the turn into Whitney's yard. "My man!" Keith yelled to himself. He was saved for the night!

A few weeks later, the PGA was coming to the state of North Carolina. Headlining the golf tournament was Tiger Woods and Roy McElroy. Keith was selected to escort the golfers while they played in the tournament. Keith was overjoyed considering how much he loved the game of golf. After kissing his family goodbye, Keith headed to the golf tournament that was being held in Charlotte, North Carolina. After a briefing from the PGA representatives and directors of the NCHP, Keith stopped and grabbed a meal from Chipotle. He was pretty tired from the near three-hour drive from Raleigh to Charlotte and from the briefing. Keith finally made it to his hotel suite for the week. He had spoken to his family back home, unpacked his luggage, showered and was enjoying his meal until his phone alerted him of a text message. As Keith looked over towards his phone, he saw that it was a text message from Whitney. He hadn't communicated with her since that laundry room quickie on the dryer. He slide his finger to the right to open the message from her. As he selected her text to open it, it read:

> *"Hey baby! I miss you so much! I know you're probably busy on the road working but I just wanted*

> to let you know that I am no longer jealous of your wife. My period was a bit late this month so I got a pregnancy test. Looks like I finally have something from you that I can call my own! I'm pregnant Keith!"

After reading, *"I'm pregnant"* in the text message, Keith leaned back in the recliner while he's cell phone slowly slid out of his hand…and onto the floor…

ACKNOWLEDGEMENTS

I would like to take this time thank you for reading *SEDUCTION*. I also would like to acknowledge all of my family and special friends who stuck by me during my roughest moments in life: my brother Bernard, Reginald (Reggie) Conyers, Derrick Dash, James Howell, Max Morris, the late Justine Hall and the late Greg Carson. Thank you for **never** giving up on me, even when I hit rock bottom. Thank you for giving me the fortitude I needed to believe in myself and my talent as a writer. It's because of you that I became fearless to expand my brand as a writer with this novel.

Curt

ABOUT THE AUTHOR

Curt Thomas is a graduate of Claflin University, where he earned degrees in sociology and criminal justice. A motivational speaker, writer, and entrepreneur, he is the owner of Curt Thomas Unlimited, LLC. As a speaker, he has received professional training from the Buckley School of Public Speaking as well as the world-renowned Les Brown.

Thomas is the author of eight inspirational self-help books, which reflect his passion for student and professional development. With his debut novel, *Seduction*, he has decided to expand his brand as an author in new and unconventional ways.

Currently, Thomas lives near Columbia, South Carolina.